Sarah H. (Sarah Hopkins) Bradford, Edward N Marks

Getting well : Tales for Little Convalescents

Sarah H. (Sarah Hopkins) Bradford, Edward N Marks

Getting well : Tales for Little Convalescents

ISBN/EAN: 9783337024994

Printed in Europe, USA, Canada, Australia, Japan

Cover: Foto ©Andreas Hilbeck / pixelio.de

More available books at **www.hansebooks.com**

GETTING WELL:

TALES FOR LITTLE CONVALESCENTS.

BY

MRS S. H. BRADFORD

AND OTHERS.

EDITED BY EDWARD N. MARKS.

LONDON:

JAMES NISBET & CO., 21 BERNERS STREET.

MDCCCLXXII.

CONTENTS.

	PAGE
POETICAL PREFACE, ...	vii
THE AUTHOR'S ADDRESS TO HER READERS, . . .	ix
THE EDITOR'S ADDRESS, ...	xi
TOMMY BELTON ; OR, THE BOY AND THE FAIRY, . .	5
KATIE'S DREAM, ...	17
SCENES IN A NURSERY I KNOW OF, ...	21
THE LITTLE PEASANT GIRL'S CHRISTMAS MORNING, . .	41
THE CLASS IN QUIZZICAL GEOGRAPHY, ...	43
WHAT TOM SAID, ...	55
WHAT HARRY SAID, ...	59
LITTLE DICK, ...	63
SEA-VIEW HOUSE, ...	79
MISS MUFF AND LITTLE HUNGRY, ...	117
LITTLE RAINY, ...	141
THE CHILDREN'S WARD, ...	167

PREFACE.

———◆———

DEAR Little Children, from whose pretty faces
    Illness has chased the rose of health away,
    Making a stillness in the halls and places
Where you have loved to ramble in your play ;
Sweet would it be to gather you about me,
Feeling your arms around my neck entwine,
Knowing you could not ever fear or doubt me,
With your sweet eyes fixed eagerly on mine.

Then I would tell you many a queer old story,
Sing you the songs and hymns of olden time
Which once I sang to others, who before me
Long sat to listen to my tale or rhyme ;
But they are gone ; and you—you are so many,
I cannot ever hope to see you all,
And so I send you, Willie, Sue, and Fanny,
And all the rest, these tales for great and small.

When of your play you now begin to weary,
Running to mother with a fretful look,
She'll lay her work down, and with voice so cheery,
Read you a story from my little book.
Well will it pay me, though I never meet you,
If you'll regard me as a friend most true,
And if my book, whene'er it comes to greet you,
Wins one kind thought from mother and from you.

Y Dear Little Readers,—

I feel as if I must explain to you something about the little piece in this book called "Katie's Dream." The first time I ever heard that story it was told (not in rhyme) by my minister to the Sunday-school children. I thought it was such a lovely story that the next day I wrote it in rhyme. And when I was making up the book for the half-ill and half-well little children, I put that little piece in it. After I had sent the book to the publishers, a little girl one day brought me a tiny little book. It was this same story, in much prettier verse than mine. So you see this lady had written her story in verse; my minister had read or heard it, and told it to the children in prose; and I had turned it into verse again for you.

But still I hope you will like it quite as well as if it had not passed through so many hands, and that the lady from whom I stole it without intending to do so, will forgive me.

Your friend,

THE AUTHOR.

M Y Dear Little Readers,—

Most of this little book was written by an American lady for American children. The people of America speak the same language that we do, and their manners and customs are very much like ours. Still they use many words that are very seldom used in Great Britain; and some of the words they use, though exactly like words which we use, have in America not exactly the same meaning that they have in Great Britain. My part of the work has been to alter the Tales a little—a very little—so that reading them, or hearing them read, may be as pleasing to British children as it is to American children.

With all the good wishes of the Author, I ask you to accept those of

THE EDITOR.

GETTING WELL:

TALES FOR LITTLE CONVALESCENTS.

———◆———

CONVALESCENTS is a large word to apply to little people, isn't it? It means those who are getting well from illness. What a pity it seems that so many dear little children should be ill! There are many diseases that seem particularly fond of seizing upon children. They stand by the side of the first few steps of their pathway, ready to catch them, or, as we say, to "be caught" by them.

Whooping-cough seizes them, and racks their little frames, and tears them almost limb from limb; and measles catches them, and spots their little faces, and wears them to skin and bone; and chicken-pox disfigures them; and mumps swells their cheeks, and makes them perfect frights. But worst of all,

A

and most dreaded by the mothers, is scarlet fever,
which clutches them, and, after throwing them on
their backs, and keeping them a long time in pain
and suffering, turns them to a brilliant red colour,
and then leaves them very weak and languid; while
mammas and nurses watch very carefully lest it
should catch them again, and give them what is
called a "relapse."

Now, all these little children are generally good
when they are very ill; but when they are able
to leave their beds, and go about their rooms, and
yet are not allowed to go out of doors and play,
then comes the hard time for mammas, and grand-
mammas, and aunties, and nurses.

Many of these little ones, at such times, are cross
and impatient, and not satisfied long with any one
thing. I have been many times shut up in a nursery
ull of such little nervous, restless beings, and I remember how often, when everything else has failed,
a story or a song would soothe the little impatient
ones (for *patients* is not the right term to apply to
them by any means), and make them forget longer
than anything else their imprisonment and priva-
tions.

All my own little ones are out of the nursery
now; some of my birds have taken wing and left
the nest, and some, alas! have soared away out of
my sight, till I meet them, as I hope I shall, in

heaven ; but my heart goes out to the many little convalescents in other nurseries, and to little cripples confined to beds or chairs ; some of whom, perhaps, have no one to tell them stories or sing them songs.

And I have thought that, though I may never see their little troubled or patient faces, and may never take them in my arms and rock them and sing to them, or tell them stories, yet that I may be so happy as to reach them through other means, and while away a few of the tedious hours of confinement to the nursery, by sending my little stories and songs to them there.

And so, dear little children all, hoping that the bloom may soon return to your cheeks, and the brightness to your eyes, and that your days of suffering may teach you lessons of patience, and of sympathy for other suffering little ones, I will proceed to tell you my first story.

TOMMY BELTON;

OR, THE BOY AND THE FAIRY.

OMMY BELTON was just getting well of the scarlet fever. He had been ill a long time, it seemed to him months, though it was only weeks, and he was now weak and nervous; more than that, he was restless, impatient, selfish, and cross.

His kind mother seldom left his side. No sooner did he express a wish for anything than she hastened to gratify it, if it were in her power. All her days were spent in ministering to him when he was very ill, and in trying to amuse him and to make the time pass less tediously when he was recovering.

It *was* rather hard for Tommy, I confess. He was alone. There had been little brothers and sisters, but they were all dead; and this was one reason why his mother looked upon him with such peculiar tenderness. He was her only one now, and she could not bear to deny him a single thing upon which his heart was set. The little children of the neighbourhood could not come to play with him, for their mothers were afraid of the disease, and so he was left to worry himself and his dear patient mother.

One night, after an unusually restless, impatient day, when Tommy's wishes had been almost as many as the minutes, and his whims constantly changing, this poor mother, having arranged all things comfortably for the night, and having assured herself that Tommy was asleep, threw her tired frame on the bed opposite to him, with her face turned towards him so that she could see him the moment he stirred, and she was soon in a very sound slumber.

She had not slept long when she was aroused by Tommy's fretful tones.

" Mother ! *mother !* "

" What is it, my son ? " was the instant reply, as she sprang from her bed.

" I 'm *hungry.* "

" Well, darling, here are some of those nice cakes, and this delicious jelly Mrs Arnold sent you ; and here are splendid grapes and oranges."

" Oh, I don't want sweet things ; I want something *solid*—codfish and potatoes ! That 's just what I want, and nothing else ! "

" *Codfish and potatoes,* my son! why the codfish is in the attic, all dry, and there is no fire, and there are no potatoes boiled. Can't you wait till morning, Tommy?"

"No, I can't! I'm *starved,* and I know how good that would taste. Nothing has tasted good since I've been ill. I've had nothing but nasty slops and sweet things. I must have some codfish and potatoes!"

"But I cannot leave you so long alone, Tommy. It will take a great while, perhaps two hours."

"Call Maria to stay with me."

"Maria has been very hard at work all day, and she has gone to bed so tired, I dislike to wake her. Do take something else, my dear boy, and have patience till morning."

Then Tommy began to lament and moan. "He could *never* have anything he wanted; he was *so* hungry—*so* hungry. No one cared whether he starved to death or not. Oh! he should die of hunger!"

At last the poor mother, seeing that there would be no rest till this unreasonable demand was complied with, said, "Well, Tommy, I will try!"

So she went and woke up Maria to come and sit with Tommy; then she went down and made up the kitchen fire; then she went up into the attic, and brought down a piece of codfish and

put it to soak ; then she went to the cellar, and
brought out some potatoes, and put them on to
boil.

Just at this time Maria appeared to say that
Master Tommy sent word, " Don't forget the eggs
and the fresh butter."

It was nearly two hours before all was done
and brought to Master Tommy, who took a wee
bit on the end of a fork, and turning away,
said, " It did not taste as nice as he thought it
would ; he had been kept waiting so long that he
did not care about it now. Besides, he was just
falling nicely asleep, and he wished they had not
disturbed him !"

The poor mother, with a sigh, set down the
plate, and went and lay down again, in the hope
of getting a little rest before morning, to prepare
her for the trial of another worrying day with
Master Tommy.

Wasn't *this* a nice boy ? Did you ever know
any one at all like him ?

All was now silent in the room. Tommy's
frettings had gradually sunk away into an indis-
tinct murmur, and finally ceased, and then his
mother fell into a sound sleep.

Tommy lay on his back, with his feet drawn
up so that his knees made a sharp little mountain
in front of him, when suddenly a wee creature

sprang up and perched herself on one of his knees. She was very, very tiny, so that he did not feel her weight any more than he would that of a butterfly.

She had a funny little cap on her head, with the point falling over and ending in a tassel, and her nose and mouth nearly met, so that her face was a good deal like that of Mistress Judy, the wife of Punch, if you have ever seen that distinguished female.

Settling herself with a little hitch on Tommy's knee, she held up one little slender finger to attract his attention, and shaking it at him in a threatening manner all the time, she began: —

"Now, see here, bad boy! Aren't you ashamed of yourself, to lie there fret, fret, fretting yourself and your poor dear mother to death? It isn't so much matter for *you;* it's a pity you hadn't died while you were so ill. I'm sure no one would have missed you (yes, every one in the house would have *missed* the trouble you gave), but no one would have mourned for you but your poor mother there; and it would have been all the better for her if you had died; she would have had a little rest then. Look at her thin pale face; nearly worn out she is, waiting on you, running for you, trying to amuse you.

"Ugh! I can't bear such selfish boys! I love

good boys. Now, look here! Down at the end of
this street there's a garret with a steep roof ; and
there lies a little boy, oh! so ill; and there he
has lain for months ; and he is alone all day,
because his poor mother must go out to work.
The garret is very hot, for the sun beats down
there tremendously, and the poor boy cannot read,
and he has no playthings, or playmates, or pictures,
or anything nice. He lies and watches the big
spiders up in the rafters, and tries to turn his poor
pale face away when they come spinning down, for
he doesn't like spiders on his face. And the flies
buzz round him, and he can't put up his weak thin
hand to drive them away, it tires him so. He has
fever sometimes, but he can hardly lift the cup of
water that his poor mother places by his side, and
when he does, it is so warm. He doesn't have ice
as you do, you fretful boy.

"Ough! I'd like to take the ice away, and
send the flies and the spiders—*swarms* of 'em—and
see what you'd do then! Now I and my little
troop fly round this poor good boy, and we fight
with the flies, and tap the big spiders on their
legs with our little wands. They are great cowards,
the spiders, and they spin up to their crannies in
the rafters, like a streak of lightning. Then we
fly over his poor face, and fan it with our little
wings, and he turns it towards the window and

thinks a little breeze is coming. Oh, I like that good, patient boy! I wish I could take him some of this nice jelly—and, dear me, *grapes!* If I could only take him *one* now, how glad I should be! *Oranges!* I wish I could roll one down the street, and hoist it up to the poor boy's window.

"*Codfish* and *potatoes!* Ough! I heard you fretting. I saw the poor mother wake up from her sleep, and go and work for two mortal hours, to get ready that meal which you wouldn't eat when it came. Oh! I'd like to take care of you! *Codfish* and *potatoes!* Much of *that* you'd get in the middle of the night! Do you know this great city is full of poor little suffering children, who have to lie and suffer, because no one has time to attend to them?

"Listen, bad boy!" (and here the little finger shook harder than ever) "your mother'll be in her grave soon, and you will have sent her there! and then who will cook your codfish and potatoes in the middle of the night? Oh, you very selfish bad boy, I'd like to *knock* you!"

And here she lifted up her tiny little wand, and stooping over, made a blow at him, at which he started; his foot gave a sudden jerk, and down hopped the fairy, as quickly as she had hopped up.

"Why—why—where is she?" exclaimed Tommy, looking over the side of the bed.

" What 's the matter, dear ?" asked his mother.

" Where did she go to, mother ?"

" You 've been dreaming, Tommy—there 's been no one here."

Tommy said nothing, and his mother went to sleep again ; but Tommy lay and thought, sometimes looking across at the pale thin face of his kind mother in the opposite bed. His mouth was dry ; he wanted a drink of water ; but he did not call to her now. " Poor tired mother," he said, " I will let her sleep;" so he helped himself to a drink, and went to sleep again.

His mother slept very late that morning, but he did not call to her as usual, to hurry and wash his face, and brush his hair, so that he might have his breakfast. Now he lay very still, thinking over all that the little creature had said to him in the night. At last a stream of sunshine burst in, and woke up the poor mother.

" Why, Tommy dear, are you awake ? what time is it ?" she asked.

" Past eight o'clock, mother—I heard the clock strike."

" Oh, why did you let me sleep so, darling ? Haven't you wanted me ? "

" I could do very well, dear mother ; and you were so tired I was glad to have you rest. I am so sorry, mother, I was so selfish in the night, in asking you to get up and cook that codfish for me : it was very wrong."

"Oh, that was no matter, Tommy. I should have been very glad to do it, if it had been any comfort to you."

"Yes, that is the worst of it, mother—I never touched it after all your trouble. Please forgive me, dear mother, and I will try to be a better boy in future."

"Why, *Tommy!* what has come over you?" asked his mother.

Then Tommy told his mother the whole story of the fairy's visit in the night.

"What a strange dream, Tommy! I'll tell you how it came to you. You remember I was reading you a fairy story yesterday?"

"Yes, mother, and then before I fell asleep, I was thinking how wrong it was to give you so much trouble; and in the afternoon I heard Jane telling Maria about poor little Nicky Price, and how his mother had to go out to work, and leave him."

"And so, altogether, that made your dream, Tommy."

"But it was just like life, mother. That little old fairy sat there right on my knee, and she held up her little finger, just so, and shook it at me ; and oh, how she *did* scold ! but I thank her for it, for I believe it has done me good. Mother, when I get well may I go and see Nicky Price, and take him some good nice things ? "

"Yes, Tommy; and if you choose, Maria may go to-day, and carry him some, and say you sent them."

"Yes ; and every day, mother ? "

"Yes ; every day, if you choose."

"And all the other sick little children, mother, who will take nice things to them ? "

"Oh, my darling boy, you are getting on to a subject that is perplexing wiser heads than yours and mine—how all the suffering and poverty in this great city is to be relieved. There are many societies, and many good people at work trying to relieve the wants of the sick and suffering, and there are hospitals and asylums, but many, very many have never yet been reached. There are so many people who never think of anything but their own pleasure and comfort, and who never give a thought to their suffering fellow-creatures."

"Yes, people just like me," said Tommy. "Well, all I can say is, I wish my old fairy would go and seat herself on each one of their knees, and give them such a *talking-to* as she gave me to-night. If *that* wouldn't wake 'em up I don't know what would ; one thing is pretty certain, I shan't forget her in a hurry."

Whether the benefit Tommy derived from the

fairy's visit was permanent or not, remains to be seen, for Tommy is still a little boy.   Selfishness is not often cured in a night, even by a visit from a fairy ; but I think we will all admit that this fairy's views of the duty of convalescent children were very sound, and that all such little ones might, if they would, learn a lesson from the scolding she gave to little Tommy Belton when she paid him a visit in the silence of the night.

KATIE'S DREAM.

IT was a sultry summer afternoon,
    And the great school-room very close and
      warm,
When little Katie's weary, tangled head
    Fell down upon her open book and arm.

And Katie dream'd—and little Willie came
    (Her little brother, who to Heaven had gone),
And press'd his face to hers, and call'd her name,
    With many a loving and endearing tone.

And she had kiss'd his little rosy cheek,
    Whose pretty laughing dimples still were there,
Look'd in his lovely deep-blue eyes once more,—
    Play'd with the ringlets of his sunny hair.

"Stay with me, Willie, darling boy!" she cried,
    "For though the angels are so bright and fair,
I love you more than they, or all beside,—
    O Willie, dear, do not stay always there!"

B

Just then a sudden noise sounds through the room,
  And on her ear the teacher's voice then broke,—
"Children, a storm is rising!   Hasten home!"
  Willie went back to Heaven, and Katie woke.

She rubb'd her eyes, and then came pouring down
  Hot tears upon her flush'd and fever'd cheek :
"Why, what's the matter, dear?" said little Bell;
  But Katie only sobb'd, and could not speak.

At length she said : "O Bell! my Willie came,
  But now I know it only was a dream,
For mother says he'll never come to us,
  Though some day we shall go away to him."

"Why *don't* you go to see him, then?" said Bell.
  "Why, dear, I do not know the way;
You know I was so very ill myself,
  I could not tell where they all went that day."

"Then *I* can tell you, darling, where he's gone ;
  I watch'd them till they turned into the gate."
"What! Heaven's gate?" said Katie. "Oh, let's run
  And find dear Willie ere it be too late!"

Then hand in hand the eager children sped,
  To find the gate of Heaven and little Will ;
The rain beat down upon each curly head,
  But only made them run the faster still.

" There, *that's* the place!" said Bell, as upward rose
    The cemetery's heavy iron gate ;
" Now hurry, Katie, hurry, for you know
    Our mothers will be worried if we're late."

" Oh dear, oh dear! how dreary it does seem,"
    Tears with the rain-drops running down her face :
" Dear Katie, I could never, never dream
    That Heaven was such a *very* dismal place."

The rain still beat on Katie's curly head,
    As loud she knock'd, and louder than before ;
" Willie, dear Willie, sister Katie's here,
    Please bring the key, and open Heaven's door."

" *I* hear him, Bell!   I hear his little feet!"
    And smiles broke o'er her face like sun through
       cloud.
" No, dear, 'tis but the pattering rain-drops' beat."
    " Well, now I'll call him very, *very* loud."

" *Willie!*" the little piercing voice then cried,
    With half a sob, and half a panting shriek ;
" Dear Willie, come! sister's so wet and tired,
    Waiting to kiss your pretty little cheek."

" Perhaps he's playing with the angels, dear,
    And does not know when you his name repeat."
" No, *now* he's coming *sure!* for well I hear
    The pretty patter of his baby feet."

"No, no, he does not come—O little Will!
 How long you leave me standing in the rain.
Bell, you must go—but I will wait here still,
 For I can never find the way again."

.   .   .   .   .   .

At length came those who long had search'd, and
 late,
 For Katie through the darkness and the storm :
Down on the ground, close by the grave-yard gate,
 They found the little senseless prostrate form.

He did not come to her—but she had gone
 To him, where there is no more cloud nor sin ;
And through Earth's darkness, gloom, and pelting
 storm,
 Katie had found Heaven's gate—and enter'd in.

.   .   .   .   .   .

From thee, sweet Katie, may we learn aright,
 Not at Death's door to seek the way to light ;
For not to sight, but unto *Faith* 'tis given,
 To find the golden gate that leads to Heaven.

SCENES IN A NURSERY.

GROUP of little convalescents were gathered together in a nursery ; five of one family. They had all, except the baby, been ill one after the other; some very ill. The eldest little girl, Katie, had lost all her pretty curls, and her head had been shaven, so that she was obliged to wear caps, which was a great mortification and. trial to her.

Next came the only boy of the family, who was called by everybody who knew him, out of the house and in it, "the Judge." This was from his remarkable likeness to his grandfather, Judge Gaston, who was a very prominent man, and much esteemed in the place where they lived. Hardly any one knew that the little boy's name was Frank ; every one spoke to him and of him as "the Judge," and when they wished to distinguish him particularly, they spoke of him as "little Judge Graham."

Next to the Judge was flighty, restless little Nell, never still for a minute, flitting about like one of the little yellow spring butterflies. She had a pretty quick temper of her own, too, had little Nell, as the other children knew to their cost sometimes.

Then there was mischievous little Fan, who was never happy long unless she was doing something that she knew she ought not to do. Last of all came "the Baby," who had never been ill, and was a perfect little ball, just trying to toddle about on very unsteady little feet.

It was a perfect Babel, that nursery, at the time of which I am writing. The chairs were all stretched across the room to make a train of carriages, of which the Judge was engineer, con-ductor, breaksman, whistle, and everything else.

The little girls, with their dollies, were the passengers, and all they had to do was to sit still and be on their good behaviour.

The engineer made enough noise for any railway train; whistling, stopping, calling out the names of places, with a strange disregard of their geographi-cal relation to each other, and then chut, chut, chutting off again. The ladies inside chatted and laughed, and admired the scenery through which they were passing.

"*Dover!*" shouted the conductor; "ten minutes for refreshments, ladies. We're going very nicely now—be in York to dinner. Ah! here's another passenger," as Nursey brings the Baby and puts her in Katie's lap. "Baggage, ma'am? tickets? all right! all aboard! *who-o-o-o-o-o-o!* chut-chut-chut," and off they are again. "*Liverpool!*" next shouts the conductor; "*London! Margate!* ten minutes at each place for refreshments."

Here Katie tried to correct some very plain geographical errors, and a stormy time ensued. The conductor "knew his own business, and wouldn't be set right by any one, especially by an old *bald-head* like *her!*"

This touched poor Katie in a very tender point. She burst into a terrible fit of crying, and insisted upon discontinuing her journey there and then; and out she got at Margate.

Then furious little Nell struck in: "Aren't you ashamed of yourself, Judge Graham? you're as unkind as ever you can be. What'll you do when the *bears* come, I'd like to know? Don't you mind him, Katie; I wouldn't cry for him."

"What do you mean by *bears?*" asked the surly Judge.

"Why, don't you know when people call other people 'bald-heads,' *bears* come and eat 'em? *Forty-two bears!* Don't you know anything about the Bible? Don't you remember the picture mamma showed us last Sunday, and the story she told us?"

"There wasn't forty-two — there was only *two*, and I could shoot them easily," said the valiant Judge. "I'd take papa's double-barrelled gun — pop! goes one gentleman; pop! goes the other — *then* where would your bears be, missis?"

"Ah, but maybe you couldn't hit 'em, and then where would *you* be, Mr Judge Graham?"

"I'd tell the bears to step into the nursery, and there they'd find two little girls in a trundle-bed — they like to eat little girls better than they do little boys."

"Ah! but we didn't say 'bald-head,' mister. They never eat anybody else."

This was a poser to the Judge, who seemed a little uneasy, but calling out "All right!" he mounted on his seat. Nell and Fannie refused positively to continue the journey unless Katie did; the conductor refused to refund their money or to give them their baggage; then there was a general scratching fight, which Nursey succeeded in quieting at last, when the Judge, again mounting his seat, started his train, and went off alone in his glory.

Bed-time came, and our little Judge began to show signs of internal tremor. He lingered in the nursery, making every possible excuse for remaining, while Nursey waited, candle in hand, urging him to go to bed, as it was long past his hour.

His room was a small one at the end of the hall, one door opening into the hall and another into the nursery.

At length, when there was no longer any excuse for delay, he started off very boldly, with long steps, toward his little room, giving, however, a scared, hasty glance over his shoulder. After all, there was a mere *possibility* of the bears.

He would not for the world have his sisters know that such an idea had entered his mind, for he knew he should never hear the last of it, and that all his superiority as the only boy of the family, the protection of his sisters and the leader in every game, would be gone entirely.

So, while he tremblingly undressed, his tone was very light and careless, and his words very brave, interspersed with an occasional whistle.

"Whew! how absurd that was, that Nell said about the *bears*, wasn't it, Nursey? I'm not afraid of any bears. Whew! they never could get *in*, could they? Besides, bears never come into *cit*— was that a *city* where the forty-two bears came and ate up the two children—I mean where the two bears came and ate up the forty-two children—was that a city, do you know, Nursey?"

Nursey's knowledge of the subject not being equal to the demand made upon it, there was no satisfactory reply. After a little pause, the Judge went on.

"Nell's such a little *dunce*, isn't she? talking 'bout *bears!* Whew! I an't afraid!—What was that noise on the stairs, Nursey?—The idea of a *boy* being afraid! Just look out in the hall, Nursey. I—I thought I saw something dark or *black* there."

"It's only your father's coat, Judge, hanging over a chair."

"Oh! only papa's coat! *that* isn't anything! You don't see anything else out there, do you, Nursey?"

"No, there's nothing else."

"You may shut the door, I think, Nursey; it's rather cold out in the hall. It makes me shiver."

The Judge lay down, apparently very brave, but thinking that the beating of his heart was the trotting of, at the least, forty-two bears. He kept still as long as he possibly could; but when he heard them actually bounding up the stairs, he could endure it no longer; so, springing out of bed, he made a dive for the nursery, where a little trembling figure in white roused Nursey from her sleep.

"Nursey! Nursey! *please* let me come in by you and Baby. I don't feel very well. I'm kind of shivering all over. I think I've got some sort of a ch-ch-chill."

"Bless me, Judge! you haven't been going and getting a relapse now, have you?"

"N-n-no, I think not," came from between the Judge's chattering lips; "but maybe I *have* taken a little cold."

Nursey took the little trembling figure in beside her, and he was very soon sound asleep, forgetful of bears and all other beasts of prey. As soon as he awoke in the morning, he began to beg Nursey not to let his sisters know that he had taken refuge in her bed the night before.

"They will say I was *afraid*, Nursey, when I was only cold, and didn't feel very well. *Wasn't* I cold, Nursey? *Didn't* my teeth chatter!"

"Yes, indeed they did, Judge, very much."

"Well, you won't tell, will you, Nursey?"

Nursey promised, but no one thought of Baby, who was just beginning to prattle, and no one remembered that babies will always say just the thing they ought not to say.

So, at the little breakfast-table in the nursery, Baby popped out the secret, during a pause in the gabbling of little tongues.

"Jud seep wid Baby," she lisped.

"Hold your tongue, Baby, and drink your milk!" said the Judge, his face as red as fire.

"What was it Baby said?" asked Nell.

"Jud seep wid Baby las' night."

"Oh goody! goody! goody!" screamed quick little Nell, jumping off from her chair and hopping up and down ; " He was afraid of the bears ! Judge was afraid of the bears ! and he went in with Nursey and Baby. Oh, you great baby coward! don't. you know that it's only old bald-headed pwophets that bears eat up children for ? And Katie isn't one of them. Oh dear! dear! dear! afraid of bears ! afraid of bears ! afraid of bears !"

" Awraid of bears ! awraid of bears ! awraid of bears !" echoed little Fan, also getting down from her chair, and hopping about the room.

" 'Faid o' base ! 'faid o' base ! 'faid o' base !" crowed the baby from her high chair.

Now the Judge was roaring with rage and morti- fication, and jumping down to make a dive at Nellie, he overturned the little breakfast-table ; and *then* there was a time ! The baby screamed, the Judge howled, the little girls shrieked with laughter, in the midst of which hubbub mamma appeared, with a countenance of dismay ; she succeeded, after a time, by threats and promises, in quelling the tumult.

The next day these restless young spirits pro- posed to be soldiers, and to go and fight the foes. Their uncle Philip was a soldier, and they delighted in nothing more than in hearing him tell stories of soldier life, and describe the scenes of a battle-field. So they petitioned their mamma for newspaper caps, and then they were ready. The Judge, of

course, must be the general, Katie was colonel,
Nell captain, Fan lieutenant, and the Baby, bringing
up the rear, toddled along as rank and file. To be
sure, this last was not very thoroughly drilled, and
was rather irregular in its motions, darting out occasionally after the pussy, or rolling round on the
floor whenever that motion suited her better than
walking, and indulging in other eccentricities, which
occasionally called for a sharp reprimand from the
officer in command.

This gentleman, acting in the double capacity of
general and drummer-boy, had his hands full, while
each of the officers was also a member of the band,
being provided with a comb and a piece of newspaper each, and so they marched off to the war to
the tune of "Rule, Britannia," their movements being
somewhat embarrassed by those of the rank and
file, who seemed to take the order "*fall in!*" to
mean "*fall down!*" and who accordingly did so,
and the whole corps were delayed till her cries were
quieted, and she put in marching order again. At
length they reached the enemy's ground, which was
supposed to be at the back of the washing-stand,
when the advancing column took up its position behind the cradle, watching a favourable moment for
an onset.

"If that young private doesn't stop bobbing in
and out in this style, she'll be picked off by some

of the enemy's sharpshooters," whispered the general. But the young private seemed to be the bravest of the company, defying the enemy by various sallies within their lines, and at last actually storming their entrenchments single-handed, in pursuit of her pussy.

Nell and Fanny darted after her, and tumbled over each other in their haste. "Two of my men down!" said the general. "*Retail* two privates to take them to the rear."

The two privates not being at hand, they scrambled up and took their position behind the cradle again. The details of this battle I will not give, except that the victory was on "our side," of course, and the enemy was driven from the field.

The next idea was to play *Hospital!* Four rows of chairs were placed along the side of the wall on which were stretched the four little girls as wounded soldiers, the Judge, you may be sure, being the visiting surgeon. Here, again, the baby was rebellious ; she wouldn't stay wounded long enough to be operated on, but would keep getting up and rolling off her chair, and toddling about independently of all hospital rules and regulations.

"Ah!" said the surgeon, coming up to Katie's cot and examining her carefully, "this is a very bad case indeed ! a very bad case indeed ; but cheer up, my fine fellow ! we 'll have your legs and arms off

in no time, and then you'll be as well as ever.
Something seems to be wrong with your head, too.
Lost all your hair, I see. After we get over this
little matter of the arms and the legs, I advise you
to get a wig." Here the arms and legs flew round
in a manner that proved them not to be entirely
useless yet, and the surgeon made a sudden wheel
towards the next cot.

"This poor man! dear me! shot through the
face! Well, I think we must take off your nose
and ears, and take out your eyes. While we're
about it, I think it would be the cheapest way to
take your head right off—it won't hurt much, my
boy! be over in a minute. What's that you say?
You'd like a few oranges first? Well! well! I'll
consult with the cook."

"This man," said the surgeon, coming to little
Fan's cot, "seems to be injured in the back. Ah
yes, my boy! There's nothing to be done but to
take out his back-bone. Don't be worried, my
brave boy. I'll fit a stick right in that'll do just as
well. I do these little things very quickly. You'll
be all right soon."

"Won't you please to *scwape* my bone and put it
back again, Doctor?" said Fan.

"Well, I'll see—I'll see," said the surgeon gravely.
"It *has* been done; in fact, I have done it myself.
I will see what *condition* your bone is in, first."

" This individual seems to be able to get about,"
said the surgeon next, as he came to the fourth cot.
But he must have had some very *ignorant* surgeon
to attend to his legs.   They have been mended very
queerly.   See how unsteadily he walks.   Oh, this
will never do—this will never do!   I must break
his legs again.   Don't mind it, my boy.   You'd
like to have better legs than these, I am sure.   To-
morrow I will just break your legs for you!"

" *Bwake my leg?* " asked Baby, sticking out one
little foot and pulling up her dress till she showed
one little dimpled knee; " no, Jud san't bwake Baby
leg."

" Ah! but, my boy, you'll soon see who is master
here.   Look at the other brave fellows there ; they
will all bear these operations like men.   Remember
you're a soldier of the *glorious British army!*
You musn't mind a little pain."

But Baby was toddling off long before the surgeon
had finished his speech, singing a little song as she
went.

An operation in dentistry was the next thing proposed by these restless young spirits, but it ended
very suddenly and very unfortunately.   The Judge
again was the principal character.   Nell came in
with her face bound up, and moaning with the
toothache.

" Sit down, my little girl!   I shan't hurt you!

not a bit! not a bit! Let me see, which tooth is
it? Ah, there are several there, twenty-five at the
least, to come out." (The Judge, you see, never did
things on a small scale.)

"I think I shall have to give you the gas," he
continued ; and seizing a pillow from the bed he
put it under his arm, and began to pump with all his
might. Nellie's eyes closed, and her mouth opened
at the dentist's command. He seized the tongs,
and plunged them in her mouth. Unfortunately
Nursey had just used them, and they were still
quite hot.

Nellie shrieked ; but the Judge, supposing that
was only a nice piece of acting, held on to her head
with one hand, and kept the tongs in her mouth
with the other, till, in her frantic struggles, she
got out of his hands, but with her poor mouth all
blistered inside.

Her screams of pain brought up her poor mother
again, who certainly thought, and with good reason,
that such a set of children as hers was never seen in '
any other nursery. It was a long time before poor
Nellie could eat with comfort, or before her mouth
recovered from the effects of the Judge's operation
in dentistry.

There seemed to be no end to the contrivances of
these children in making amusement for themselves
and trouble for others. Among other pretty toys

sent to them during their illness was a beautiful
lamb as large as life, on wheels. It was made so
strong that one of the children could get on its back
and be drawn about the nursery.

But at length they grew dissatisfied with it as it
was originally, and began to wish that it was black.
"We can't sing 'Ba! ba! black sheep!' to it at all,
because it's white," they said.

"Well," said the Judge, "let's *make* him
black!"

"How?" asked the eager little girls.

"How? why, easy enough," said the Judge;
"we can *paint* him!"

"But we haven't paint enough. These little
cakes of black paint in our boxes wouldn't be a
quarter enough."

"*I'll* tell you," said Nell; and looking round to
see if Nursey were listening, she put her hand up
to hide her mouth, and whispered, "Papa's big ink
bottle!"

"Good for Nell!" said the Judge. "Just the
thing! But how shall we get it?"

"I'll get it for you," said Nell. "Wait till
Nursey goes down to her dinner."

Accordingly the large bottle of ink was quietly
smuggled under Nell's apron, to the children's great
delight.

The Judge undertook to pour the ink on the

lamb, but he did it as he did everything else, in too great a hurry. Down came a big river of ink over the lamb's back ; the woolly covering would not retain it, and off ran the black stream, making a great pool on the carpet.

"Oh dear! oh dear! what shall we do? Mamma will punish us, I know."

"*Us!* said the Judge ; "you *perposed* it."

"And Nell brought it," said Katie ; "but you poured it on, Mr Judge. If you had only been a little careful, it wouldn't have gone over the floor."

Katie had gone down upon her knees, and was sopping up the ink with her apron and dress, thus making matters a great deal worse. These last words brought on a general fight, in which the ink was pretty equally distributed over all the clothes and faces.

What a sight for Nursey as she opened the door with Baby in her arms!

"Oh, you *bad*, NAUGHTY, WICKED children! What will your mamma and papa say to *this*, I should like to know. I shall call them both directly up to see this sight." And down went Nursey, while the children stood and stared at each other in dismay.

Very soon they heard steps ascending the stairs, and presently their parents stood in the nursery door. The mother gave only a sigh of despair.

" What can be done with these children ?   I am
utterly and entirely discouraged ! " said the poor
mother.

" Well, I 'll tell you," said the father.   " Just
as long as you keep them shut up here, they
will be in mischief.   They *are* active, busy little
creatures, and very likely they do not intend to
do harm, but only to find amusement for themselves."

" Yes, papa ! that 's just it—we never meant to
let the ink go on the floor—we were only making
our lamb into a ' Ba ! ba ! black sheep.' "

" Well, mamma, you had better let them run in
the park ; the days are warm and bright, and they
are quite well."

" Oh, I wish I could, I am sure ; but I am so
afraid of a relapse."

" There is no danger—let them go."

But the mother said she would wait just one week
more, and then they might go out of doors.   The
little ones were delighted with their escape ; and
they were truly sorry for the mischief they had
done when they saw how much trouble they had
given their dear mother and Nursey, who had to
take up the carpet, and scrub it, and at last take it
to pieces, and re-make it, putting the soiled part
under the bed.

I wish I had nothing worse to tell you of these

unfortunate young people, but there is one more
sad tale to tell before I finish.

Their uncle had sent them a pretty little shaggy
dog whose name was Hector. This little dog was
a great amusement to the children, but it seemed
as if they could not play long with anything without getting into trouble.

The Judge was climbing to the top of a wardrobe
one day, in search of some playthings, when he discovered a box in which were some fire-crackers, left
from last November.

" Oh, what fun ! Let's take these crackers and
tie them to Hector's tail, and set them off and see
him run !"

" Oh no !" said Katie, " it will hurt him."

" No, it won't, you goosey !" said the Judge.
" I mean to make a long string of crackers, and tie
them with a piece of twine to his tail. It will only
make him run."

No sooner said than done. The time was
chosen when Nursey and Baby were down at their
tea. The crackers were safely tied on while one of
the children was feeding Hector with a piece of
meat, and then a match was lighted and applied to
the last cracker. Crack ! crack ! crack ! went the
reports. The poor little dog started off in terror,
and dashed about the room in a frantic manner,
running up against little Fan, whose apron and

dress were in a moment blazing. Katie rushed into the hall and pulled the bell with all her might, screaming, "Mamma! Nursey! come! come quick! Fire! fire! Do come! Fannie's burning!"

The Judge, like a little coward, scampered away too, leaving only Nell with poor little Fan, who was screaming with pain and fright.

All this took but a moment. Mamma and Nursey came rushing up-stairs. Fortunately the Baby's bath stood in the nursery nearly filled with warm water. Nursey seized little Fan and plunged her in, so that she escaped with only a few slight burns; then the Judge returned, and seizing the little dog, whose tail was already smoking, plunged him in beside her, and so fortunately the flames were all extinguished without any serious injury. But the children had a great fright that time. I think it might possibly have done them good and made them less mischievous, even if the doctor, for whom their mamma had sent, had not given it as his opinion that they might safely go out into the park and play.

Oh, what a happy set of children they were when they gained their freedom once more! but not more so, I think, than their parents and poor Nursey, who sat under the trees with her knitting and watched them playing where they could not very easily hurt themselves, or anything else. No one but those who have long been confined to the house after weeks of illness can realise how happy these little active beings were. They rolled and tumbled over the grass, drove horses, rolled hoops, skipped, and grew fat and ruddy every day.

I hope these children will not be taken as *examples* by other children who read of their mischievous doings. Children may be funny, and bright, and clever, without doing one bit of mischief ; and I hope my " little convalescents," to whom I am writing, will never cause the trouble that these little ones did.

THE LITTLE PEASANT GIRL'S CHRISTMAS MORNING.

I AM a little peasant girl,
  My father's very poor ;
No rich or handsome things have we,
  No carpet on our floor.

Last night I hung my stocking up,
  As other children do :
Dear father put an apple in,
  Mother a cake or two.

But, oh! this morning when I woke,
  I saw, with wondering eyes,
Four pretty pictures in my room,
  Alike in form and size.

Hills, waterfalls, and lakes were there,
  With forests circling round,
Through which there came some frighten'd deer
  Pursued by many a hound ;

Cities, and spires, and hamlets fair,
  And temples tall and grand,
With winding rivers running near
  By lofty bridges spann'd.

And merry boys come gliding down
    The tall hill's snowy side;
While on the smooth and glassy lake
    Others in circles glide.

Oh! none can tell with what delight
    I lie and fondly gaze
Upon my picture, sparkling bright
    In morning's early rays.

Who gave them to me, do you ask?
    And how much did they cost?
The giver I have never seen—
    The painter is *Jack Frost.*

I would not change my little home
    For any rich man's store;
For, oh! his children cannot know
    The *pleasures of the poor!*

You do not see these pretty sketches, dear children, made by the fairy fingers of Jack Frost, because your nurseries are warm, and his work has melted away so often that he has given up trying to make pictures for you. So, you see, though you have a good many pretty things that the little peasant girl cannot have, God takes care that she shall have *some* pleasures, and so He sends her the beautiful frost-work pictures.

THE CLASS IN QUIZZICAL GEOGRAPHY.

IT was a rainy day, and a number of bright, lively, active children were shut up together in an old house in the country, where they were spending the summer with their parents.

It is a very hard thing for children to be made prisoners in this way, and to be thrown upon themselves and each other for amusement. There is no going to the stream for fish, or to the barn to play in the hay, or to the orchard for apples. They are far from neighbours, and cannot hope to visit or be visited. Some children under such circumstances will stand flattening their noses against the window panes, watching the down-pour of the rain, fretting over the state of the weather, and wishing a thousand times in the day that it would clear off. But these children were bright, pleasant little creatures, and the ruling spirit among them, Ruby Ray, was full of ingenious contrivances for the amusement of the rest; and could keep them happy and contented through a week of rainy days by her wonderful

powers in the way of story-telling, and by her endless variety of games, and plays, and fun, and
frolic.

Ruby was the oldest of the six, and she was only
seven years old. She was the leader, director, mother,
schoolmistress, preacher, chorister — in short, the
most prominent character was always Ruby's, and
the others submitted as a matter of course, never
dreaming of aspiring to her place. The whole party
soon repaired to the large old attic, which was their
favourite resort on rainy days. And is there a
pleasanter sound to be heard than that of the rain
"pattering on the roof," when you are all secure, and
safe, and comfortable inside ?

One end of this old attic, where the windows
were, was partitioned off into several little rooms,
all now empty. Here they brought their dolls, and
rags, and silks, and bits of broken china, and each
young lady established herself in a different room,
where she went to housekeeping, and was ready to
receive the visits of her friends, which were very
promptly returned.

And what wonderful rag-babies these little girls
made! The bodies were one straight roll of cotton,
sewed up tightly ; the legs were two smaller rolls,
fastened to the large roll ; the feet two other little
rolls, sticking out at right angles from the legs, and
the arms were made of one long roll, sewed across

the back and extending out straight on each side. With a little paint-box and a brush, hair, eyes, cheeks, and lips were soon manufactured to order ; and I venture to say, no little girl ever enjoyed her elegant wax doll, dressed in silks and satins and laces, more than these little girls did their large families of rag-babies, of all shapes and sizes, which they contrived and dressed for themselves.

"Indeed, I must have a nurse for these children," said Ruby. "Where's Jet? Jack, go down and tell Jet to come to me directly."

"Jet" was a little negress, rightly named, if her name was intended to represent her outward appearance, for a more shining little darky never made her way from the regions of the sunny South. Her real name was Jetalina, and was given her by a romantic young lady in the family of her former mistress.

Her mother, who was now cook in this country-house, had come not long before from bondage as a slave in South America, and Jet was happy to be the plaything or the servant, whichever might suit them, of the little white ladies up-stairs. At the summons of Jack, her little bare feet were soon heard pattering up the stairs, after which the rolling of her white eye-balls were presently seen.

In one part of the attic the two older boys, Freddy and Jack, had set up a carpenter's shop with some old tools, some blocks, and long nails, which they found lying about.

Here they made tables and chairs for the large family of dolls, and with bits of broken china for dishes, they were soon ready to give an entertainment. Jet waited at table, as happy to serve as the others were to be served; and so the happy children amused themselves throughout the hours of the rainy day.

"Oh, dear, if I only had three pins!" exclaimed Ruby, as she was preparing the larger ones of her family for a walk.

"Take 'em out of Jet's wool," says Fred; "it's full of 'em."

"Jet, you don't really carry pins round in your hair?"

"Sure I does, Miss Ruby, jes' dig you fingers in, an' you'll fine 'em plenty. Ole missis use to say, 'Jet an't good for nuffin, on'y two fings. Allers has pins in her wool, an' I can allers wipe my fingers on it when dey's greasy and crocky.'"

"Did she really wipe her fingers on your wool, Jet?"

"Allers, missy," said Jet, who was busily working in her wool, and extracting a pin at every dive.

"Oh, look! here's ten!" exclaimed Ruby. "Are there any more, Jet?"

"Lots, I guess, missy. Here's noder, here's noder—here's two noders."

"Twenty!" shouted Ruby.

"Go on, Jet," put in Jack, "let's see how many you can find."

Jet worked away; the result was forty-two pins!

"Now I guess zou's got 'em all, missy," says Jet. "'Specks dere's more down yer were de wool's so tick, on'y I can't get at 'em. Now you's done got all my pins. I'll have to go hunt up more."

"Did your old missis ever whip you, Jet, like they did Topsy in 'Uncle Tom?'"

"Whip me, missy?" said Jet, who was utterly ignorant of Topsy and her sufferings. "Guess you'd better! pokers, tongs, butter-ladle, anything she lay her hand on—crack! crack! all day long;" and Jet picked up a doll's dress, and examined it admiringly, saying, in the same breath, "Laws! an't 'em bu'ful?"

"What did Susanne say to that?" (Susanne was Jet's mother.)

"Oh, Susanne! she could'n do nuffin. Whip Susanne too—tie her up—did'n *she* holler! Then one day, Pomp he say, Massa Linkum come, an' we's free; an' Susanne an' me, we cut."

In the afternoon, the children began to be
dull and fretful, and the boys proposed going off
down-stairs, when Ruby, always ready, called
out—

"Oh, look here, children! let's have a school.
I'll be schoolmistress, and you'll be scholars.
Here's my stick, and here's just the thing for a
ruler. Let's go over here by the big work-
table, and I'll stand behind like Miss Grey.
Come, all sit down—attention. Jet, Jet—what's
your last name, Jet?"

"I dunno, missy—'specks I han't got nuffin but
Jet."

"Well, sit down there. All look at me. First
class in Quizzical Geography." (Ruby meant
Physical Geography, but she was very apt to make
mistakes in hard words.)

"I don't know anything about that stuff," said
Jack.

"Never mind. *I* didn't know anything about
it either, till I heard Miss Grey teaching the big
girls. *I'll* teach you."

"But it's very necessary that I should have
a globe. Jack, uncle will do anything for you.
Go and ask him if we can't have his big globe for
a little while, for a geography class. That's a
good boy."

Jack trotted off, and in a few minutes was

heard puffing up the stairs with the great globe in his arms.

"Uncle says you must be very careful of it," said he.

"Yes, we will.—Children, look at me. This is the globe we live on."

"No, we don't live on that, neither," says Fred.

"Well, of course not on this very thing. Don't be ridiculous, Fred."

"What did you say we did for, then?" asked Fred.

"You know what I mean just as well as can be, Fred Ray, and if you don't stop interrupting you shall go down-stairs. Didn't you say the other day, when you showed Aunty your photograph, 'That's me?' Well, I mean just so when I say this is our globe."

This clear explanation was satisfactory to the whole school.

"Now, this globe of ours——If that scholar · below don't stop singing, I shall have to whip him."

Poor little Nick, who was moving backwards and forwards, and shouting, "There was an old nigger, and they called him Uncle Ned," now looked up, and shaking back his curls, said, in a sweet little pleasant voice—

"*Nit* mussen be fipped."

"Well, Nick *will* be whipped, if he doesn't stop singing so loud," said the teacher.

"Vell, den I'll stop," said good little Nick; and he sat very silent, till at last his head fell over, and he dropped asleep.

"Now, children, this is our world."

"Does our world have a brass thing round it like that?" asked Fred.

"Well—yes—I suppose it does," said the schoolmistress, who, like many another schoolmistress, thought it was best not to say "I don't know" to any question that might be asked.

"What's that line right round *there!*" asked Kitty.

"Oh, that's the *Quaker;* and each side is the *horrid zone*, all round there."

"What's it horrid for?"

"Cause it's so very dreadful hot there."

"Does dem beasts go walk round dere all de time, missy?" asked Jet, looking with interest at the signs of the zodiac on the rim supporting the globe.

"Oh, there's awful beasts down there, Jet," said Ruby.

"Do they keep going round and round and round?" asked little Hetty.

"I s'pose they do, or the globe wouldn't say so.

You mustn't ask so many questions, or we shall never get through with our lesson."

"Mr Phelps always tells us to ask all the questions we want to," said Jack. "Mr Phelps is a nice teacher. You an't a nice teacher at all!"

"Well, then, ask *decent* questions."

"*Didn't* we ask decent questions—we didn't know about the horrid zone, and the animals going round and round."

"Well, you know *now;* so be quiet. Now, children, this world of ours is only a crust like the peel of an orange, without any orange in it—only the earth is all full of burning melted fire inside."

"Crackey!" exclaimed Jack, looking on the floor, and suddenly jumping into another seat.

"Oh, you needn't move so quick, Mr Jack; the fire is under you just as much where you are now."

"Does it ever come up and burn people?" asked Kitty.

"Certainly it does, in some places, like Besubeus, and Popoty—no—Catapy—well it's of no consekens —some place, anyhow; it comes up and burns cities and towns, and all the people. Where are you going, Jack?"

"I—I dug a hole yesterday, very deep, and I'll go and pour a little water in."

"You great goose!" said Fred, "*you* couldn't dig

through. Don't they dig deeper wells every day, and don't cold water come up in 'em?"

"To be sure! *There*, Miss Rube, what do you say to that? Where's your fire now, I should like to know. I think you go a little deeper than an orange peel then. I wouldn't be a teacher and say what is not true."

"I didn't *say* it wasn't any thicker than an orange peel," said Ruby, her lip quivering; "I knew better than that; I can't explain it exactly; but Miss Grey said you could *perpare* it to the skin of an orange. The earth is a great deal bigger than the orange, and the crust is a great deal thicker—oh, miles thick!"

"Oh, that's what you're driving at, is it? Well, go ahead!"

"Pshaw! who's afraid, then?" said Jack; "that an't anything to hurt any one."

"Now, just look a-here, Miss Rube," said Fred, "China's right opposite to us, an't it?"

"Yes, I suppose so," said Rube slowly, turning the globe to see if she was right. "Yes, of course it is, *directly* opposite!"

"Well, then, when we're heads up, they're heads down, an't they? Now, just tell us how they manage that, will you?"

"I can't exactly tell you, but they do."

"'Specks dey holds on to de trees," suggested Jet.

"I think they's dot stiting-plaster on their feet," said little Hetty.

"But sometimes *we're* down, Miss Grey says, and we don't have any trouble to hold," said Ruby.

"But you know we *an't* down," said Jack.

"I use for be down," said Jet, "when ole missis catch me up by de heels, jes' for nuffin at all, on'y not feed de chickens—suffin like dat. 'Specks I was in China den, wasn't I, Miss Ruby?"

"I never *did see* such ignorant children!" exclaimed Ruby, with a sigh of despair. "There's no use in trying to teach you anything!"

"Well, it's all such humbug! I don't believe in your old Quizzical Geography! I don't believe there's any fire!—I believe it's all flat just like it is here—and I *know* we don't go heads down; *any* fool would know that!"

"You're a very bad boy, Jack, to talk so. You ought to believe everything these good geography people tell us!" said Ruby, indignantly.

"I'll believe it, Ruby; don't cry," said Kitty. "Now what does them long lines mean, running down?"

"Well, I am afraid you wouldn't understand that, dear. It's something about longitude and the Green witch that lives in England."

"Cudjo use for tell me 'bout de witches—black witches an' white witches, but he never done say

nuffin 'bout green witches. Is um any of dese tings
goin' 'roun' yer ? " asked Jet.

"No, I think not, Jet, but you are not old enough
to understand all about that yet. And I think
you may all go. There's the tea-bell ! " And so
school was out, and the rainy day was over.

WHAT TOM SAID.

I CARE for no one—no, not I ;
    I don't heed what folks say ;
I 'll do just what I please to do ;
    I 'll eat, drink, sleep, and play.
I 'm tired of doing what I 'm bid,
    I 'll show I have a will ;
I 'm treated like a baby-boy
    Because I 've been so ill.

I care not what the doctor says,
    I will not take his stuff ;
Of horrid powders, pills, and draughts,
    I'm sure I 've had enough.
The doctor only physics me
    To send papa a bill !
I think that doctors must rejoice
    When boys and girls are ill.

Don't tell me Doctor Snell is kind,
    And tries to make me well.
How kindness he has shown to me,
    I'm sure I cannot tell.
It makes me angry when I hear
    How people praise his skill;
Think of the stuff he sent, for me
    To take when I was ill.

He never ordered jams or tarts,
    Or sweetmeats, or nice fruit;
He would not let me eat rich cake—
    Such things my taste would suit.
I'll have them now—of cakes and fruit
    And sweets I'll have my fill—
All that I ask for I should have
    When I have been so ill.

And I'll go out, too, when I like;
    At home why should I stay?
I'm well enough—I'm sure I am—
    With other boys to play.
I want to walk to Dobson's farm,
    And then to Wheatley's mill;
I'm sure I ought to take long walks
    When I have been so ill.

There's no need now for taking care,
　For I am getting strong ;
I don't like always being told
　That this or that is wrong.
'Tis now great heat I must avoid,
　Then 'tis a cold or chill ;
It seems I never can do right
　Since I have been so ill.

I'm told how good I ought to be—
　What danger I was in ;
I hear enough, I'm sure, about
　Ingratitude and sin.
Of course I say what's wrong at times,
　When I'm ill-tempered ; still,
More *patience* folks should have with me
　When I have been so ill.

Don't talk to me about the care
　Which others took of me ;
It was but right when I was ill,
　As ill as I could be.
You know I had to lie in bed
　For many days, until
I told the doctor 'twas his stuff
　That made me feel so ill !

　　　　　　　　E. N. M.

WHAT HARRY SAID.

MOTHER dear, how kind you 've been!
  And so has Kitty too ;
I 'm sure I never can repay
  The debt I owe to you.
You 've sat and watched me day and night,
  Your patience none can tell ;
How very thankful I should be
  That I am getting well!

I fear I was a fretful boy
  When I was suffering so ;
I tried to keep from troubling you,
  But 'twas so hard, you know,
When every sound my head disturbed,
  Even the old church bell ;
But how I love to hear it ring,
  Now I am getting well!

I love to hear the boys at play
    Out yonder on the green,
Just where on every Saturday
    So happy I had been ;
But now you say I soon can go,
    With you and little Nell,
And round our garden take a walk,
    Because I'm getting well.

How very thankful I should be
    To God, who is so good,
Who gives me everything I have,
    My home, and friends, and food ;
Who raised me up when I was ill—
    Oh ! I can never tell
How much I owe to that kind Friend,
    Who now has made me well.

For there are many children still
    Who lie on beds of pain,
And some of them will suffer long,
    And ne'er get well again ;
How frequently for children dead
    We hear the tolling knell,
But God has eased me of my pain,
    And I am getting well.

Others have no such cheerful home
   As God has given to me,
No loving friends to watch and care,
   No pleasant things to see ;
How very thankful I should be,
   I 'm sure I cannot tell,
'Tis almost nice to have been ill,
   Just to be getting well.

LITTLE DICK.

D O you know how exceedingly cold the weather is in Western New York about the time of the holidays? Sometimes there are days and nights when the wind blows as if it were determined to force an entrance by door or window, or to take revenge by tearing off roofs and shutters, or carrying away chimneys. How it whistles, and roars, and raves round the corners of the house, with now a high shrill treble, and then a thundering bass ; now a shriek like a spirit in terror, and then a groan like one in remorse and despair!

It was on such a night as this, " the night before Christmas," six years ago, that I sat alone before my parlour fire. I had just filled three stockings—alas ! alas ! *three,* where once were *six ;* and as I sat thinking of the cluster of little heads which had gathered round that same hearth on other Christmas eves, and of all their lovely ways and pretty sayings, the time went on, and the fire went out. Still the wind raved, and whistled, and roared ; and as I knelt to say my evening prayer, I commended to our loving Heavenly Father the outcast, and the wanderer, and the sailor on the sea.

Just then I heard the door of the storm-house fly back violently, as the fierce wind caught it and hurled it nearly off its hinges, and then I thought I heard a tapping as of timid little fingers at the door. I waited a moment, almost sure that I must have been mistaken, when the knocking was repeated more distinctly. I opened the door, and the light of the hall lamp fell on as forlorn a little object as ever my eyes had seen. A poor little half-frozen boy, with tattered clothes, worn-out shoes, and no hat, his mass of tangled hair filled with snow, his little red hands unprotected by mittens, and one side of his face swollen frightfully.

This I saw at a glance, while the poor little object was saying, in tones hoarse as those of one in the last stages of croup, "Please, missis, won't you let me sleep here to-night?" "Come in! come in!" said I, for the bitter cold seemed to chill me to the marrow. He came in and stood by the great hall stove, looking at me with a half-frightened, half-pleading air, as if to beg me not to turn him out into the darkness and the storm again. Poor little miserable, filthy, homeless, houseless object! "Inasmuch as ye did it unto one of the least of these, ye have done it unto Me."

These words came into my mind; but it was more from impulse than from any dictate of Christianity, that I decided that the poor child must not go out again that night, into the "pelting of the pitiless storm."

"What is your name, my poor child?" I asked.

"Dick, ma'am."

"And where do you come from?"

"I've staid round in barns and under hedges most nights, but it's too cold to-night, and my face aches."

"I should think it *was* too cold to-night; and have you no home?"

"My mother lives over by the Marsh, but my stepfather won't let me stay there, and I an't got nowhere else to stay, and no one won't give me no work."

"Have you asked any one else to take you in to-night?"

"Yes, ma'am,—wherever there was a light in the houses; but I suppose it was the servant girls came to the door, and they shut it quick, I tell you, when they saw me, and didn't say nothing but 'Go 'long!'"

"And what do you do all day, Dick?"

"Play in the street, ma'am; it's fine fun."

To see poor little half-naked Dick, as he stood

E

shivering and chattering by the stove, one would think that fun and he had parted company long ago, and for ever.

"And do you ever steal, or say wicked words, Dick?"

"I never *steals*, ma'am. I wouldn't do it. I've been hungry many a time, but I wouldn't steal a mouthful."

"But you *do* say wicked words, do you?"

"I do what other boys does, but I don't steal."

"Did you ever hear of God, Dick?"

"Yes, ma'am, in a Ragged school, and the lady told me beautiful stories about the angels. I wish't I could *see* 'em!" (This he said with a rub of the wrist across the nose.)

"Perhaps you will, one day, Dick."

It was getting late, and it was Saturday night, and while I had been talking with Dick my mind had been revolving the question, "What *am* I to do with him, and where *can* I put him?"

It occurred to me that there was in the basement a disused bath-room, which might be converted into a temporary sleeping-place for my unexpected guest. Leaving Dick busily engaged upon a huge slice of bread and butter, and swinging his feet in token of his delight, as he sat by the great warm stove, I went down to explore and arrange, my servants and all the rest of the household being in bed.

An old mattress was drawn forth from some hidden retreat, a pillow followed, and for covering, some old but thick and warm carpets ; for nothing once used by poor little filthy Dick could ever be put to other use again. When all was ready, I conducted him to his apartment, a more sumptuous one, with a more comfortable bed, than his poor little bones had reposed in for many a long night, if ever before.

Dick looked around the room, inspected the bed, and uttering the single word *"jolly!"* threw himself down, in his rags, drew his carpet coverlet over him, and then looked up at me with a grin of intense satisfaction. But the sad side of the picture was all I saw, and my tears dropped on the old carpet which covered him as I said, " Now, Dick, you will pray to God to take care of you to-night, and to make you a good boy, will you not ? "

"Yes, ma'am," answered Dick, and probably in good faith, but the weary eyelids closed, and the boy was in the land of dreams before I left the room.

What must have been the poor child's former surroundings, to make such a bed and such a room so comfortable to him !

My Saturday night's work was not finished yet. Up in the attic was a sacred treasure—garments once worn by one who would never need earthly garment more. It was a sad task to go up late at

night, and rake up mournful memories, by bringing
these once familiar objects to light again, and thus
carrying on still further the train my thoughts had
been pursuing, before I was disturbed by the rap of
little knuckles on the door. But to what better use
could these garments be put than that of thus
literally " clothing the naked ? " And so feeling
must be sacrificed, and the precious store broken in
upon.

An entire suit was found, which would about
fit little Dick, and this was brought down, and laid
outside his door—his Christmas gift—for Sunday
morning.

And did not *He* whose lowly birth and
glorious resurrection we were on that morning to
remember with thanksgiving and praise, look
down in pity even on poor prayerless little
Dick, as he lay sleeping so snugly under his
carpet covering ? " He took upon Himself our
nature," that He might sympathise with our
sufferings.

It was a difficult undertaking to rouse little
Dick the next morning. He was making up for the
long, cold, restless nights he had spent, cramped up
in boxes, and neither knocking nor calling (for
reasons of my own I did not venture on *shaking*)
had power to rouse him for a long time. But at
length Bridget's thundering tones were brought to

bear on the sleeper, and probably imagining that it was the "Move on!" of a policeman, Dick sprang with a frightened air from his lowly bed.

When he was thoroughly awake there were a few things to be explained and understood. In the first place, it was delicately hinted that there was the old bath-tub, into which Bridget would proceed to dash several pails of water, after which, with the assistance of a good supply of soap, Dick might exercise himself therein for fifteen or twenty minutes, without injury to his physical condition.

Secondly, there were the new clothes, into which he might be inducted as soon as possible after the first process was completed.

Thirdly, the old clothes must then be made up into a bundle, and taken down through the garden gate, and thrown into the river. The bedclothes also were to be taken to the loft of the wood-house.

Fourthly, there was a good warm breakfast to be eaten, after which Dick might proceed on his way rejoicing, with a strong recommendation to proceed to the school, and then to church.

Dick's eyes glistened at secondly and fourthly, but the preliminaries did not present very strong attractions to one so much more accustomed to "*suffer*" than to "*do*."

In about an hour I went down to the kitchen,

and there sat Mr Dick, eating a hearty breakfast, and entertaining the girls, who were holding their sides while they laughed.

" Well, well!" said Bridget, "if that isn't an odd child!"

As soon as Dick saw me, he jumped up, and inspecting himself from head to foot with as much pride as ever city dandy surveyed his own person when ready for a ball, he said with an inimitable leer—

" *Now*, missis, if I only had a pair of *gloves !*"

As we were sitting in church that day, one of my children directed my looks to the gallery, and there to be sure was Dick, his smiling countenance beaming down upon us in the most condescending manner imaginable.

Nothing was heard from Dick for some weeks, when again, late one night, stormy and cold as the one of which I have been telling you, the tap of little knuckles was heard on the door, and we all exclaimed, " That must be Dick!"   And Dick to be sure it was ; the nice suit all torn and dirty, and his whole appearance nearly as forlorn as on that Christmas eve, save that he had held on to the cap,—which indeed he was *literally* now doing, to keep the wind from hurling it down the street.

" Please, missis, may I sleep here to-night ? it 's too cold to sleep out-of-doors."

Of course, the bed and the carpets must be brought down again, and once more Dick was my guest. Again in the morning he disappeared, and the next I heard the poor child had been dragged out of a packing-case or hogshead, and sent to the poor-house, fourteen miles away. In a week he was back, having walked all the way, and again, late at night, he offered himself as a candidate for a sleeping apartment.

"Why did you leave the poor-house, Dick?"

"Oh, I didn't like it there, ma'am. The coffee was *poor*, not half so good as yourn."

"Thank you for the compliment, Dick; but you had a comfortable home, and a bed to sleep on at least. It must have been better than living in the way you have lived all the winter."

"No, ma'am, not much; there was a man there named Peter that licked us boys awful; he hand't got no arms."

"Now, Dick, I am afraid you tell stories. If the man had no arms, how could he lick you as you say?"

"Why, missis, he's got a stump, and he kind o' fixes the handle of the whip under it, this way, and swings himself round, and I tell *you* it stings."

All the time Dick was swinging *himself* round on the balusters, occasionally breaking out into a whistle or a snatch of a song.

Again in the morning Dick disappeared, and the next story I heard of him was a sad one. Another boy had stolen something, and when pursued, had escaped, leaving the stolen article in Dick's hands. Dick was arrested, and in spite of his protestations, was sent away fifty miles to the reformatory. There he found a brother, who was at work in the shoe-shop, and Dick was put along with him, and was so happy that when matters were righted, and the real offender was sent up to be exchanged for Dick, the poor little fellow came away with real regret. He called on us again, and gave us the pleasure of his company for the night, and was very entertaining with his stories of prison life. The next morning a neighbour of mine gave him a little work to do, for which he paid him sixpence, charging him to keep it to buy something to eat when he was hungry. That evening I heard the most remarkable sounds from the kitchen, a kind of wheezing and scraping and whining all together, accompanied with the shuffling of feet and shouts of laughter. Descending to the region whence the sounds proceeded, I saw Master Dick seated on the kitchen table, his mouth stretched with glee, an old broken toy fiddle (for which he had bartered his sixpence) across his shoulder, and scraping away to the *time*, but not the *tune* of Auld Lang Syne, while the servants and some of their friends were dancing a double-shuffle.

" My eye ! how they do go it, missis !" said Dick, never ceasing his sawing on the poor battered imitation of a fiddle.

The next morning, after breakfast, the little vagrant went off again, and no trace of him was left but the broken fiddle, thrown down carelessly beside the front gate.

Again, one evening, the familiar tap at the door, and on opening it, I jumped back with a scream, as what appeared to be a live wriggling snake made directly for my face.

" Take care, missis ! he 'll bite you !" said a voice, in Dick's familiar husky tones.

" Where *did* you get that creature, Dick ?" I asked.

" Oh, I swept a walk, and the lady gave me sixpence."

" And you spent it for this paper snake, did you ?"

" Yes ; I see a boy have it, an' he said he 'd sell it me for sixpence, an' I went all round asking for work till I got some. An't he *pretty?* an' I 'm going round to frighten the girls in the kitchen. Don't you say nothin', missis."

Dick had begun now to look upon his bed-room and bed as a fixed institution, whenever it suited his pleasure to take possession of it. He regularly deposited the bed in the loft whenever he had used it,

and he often appeared at the kitchen door at night,
bed in arms, before the servants knew that he was
about.   But he was such a good-natured, careless,
merry little fellow, that they all began to like him,
and to hail his coming with a greeting of welcome.

One evening, when I was talking to him in the
kitchen, a woman came in with a neighbour's child
in her arms.   "Oh," said Dick, with a sort of sigh,
"I *wish't* I could see *my* little brother!"

"Have you got a little brother, Dick?"

"Yes, missis; he just begin to climb up by a
chair, and toddle round.   He's just as cunnin'!   I
wish't I could see him!"

His desire to return to his big brother in the reformatory at length became so strong, that he did
what hunger and cold had never been able to force
him to do,—he *stole*, on purpose to be caught and
sent to prison.   And thither he was sent, and for a
few months did his duties well.   But Dick did not
like work; his vagrant wanderings had unfitted
him for steady labour, and he longed for rest, and
the pleasures of an idle life again.

Two or three boys one day tasted some white
lead which was in the painters' shop, and it made
them sick, so that they were taken from work and
sent to the hospital.   Some other boys proposed to
Dick that they should do the same, and thus escape
work for a time.   But they did not know what a

deadly poison it was, and they took a great deal too
much of it, to make them " only a little sick," as they
proposed to be.

One poor little fellow died immediately. The
rest were very, very ill; their bodies swelled
frightfully, and became of a yellow sickly hue, and
their sufferings were dreadful. Dick's mother heard
somehow that her little boy was dying in the prison.
The mother's heart now triumphed over every other
feeling, and coming into the village, she took a room,
and started off to bring Dick home to die.

I heard at length that he was at home, and went
to see him. No one could recognise little Dick now.
His hair was cut close, his face pale and with the
look of death upon it, his feet frightfully swollen.

"Don't you know the lady, Dick?" asked his
mother.

He tried to say "No," but the hoarseness of death
was upon him now, and I could only judge by the
movement of his swollen and purple lips what he
intended to say.

"Don't you know me, Dick? the lady who let
you sleep at her house so many nights?"

Then his face broke into a faint smile, and he
nodded his head.

" Is there anything I can make for you, Dick,
that you would like?"

He shook his head.

"Wouldn't you like some chicken broth or jelly?"

With an effort that fairly racked his frame he gasped out, "I d-do-no how it taste, ma'am."

Poor little sufferer! Often had he longed for the dry crust which "no man gave him," and now he had no power to swallow the most delicate dainties. I took some of these nice things to him the next day, but after trying to taste them he turned away disgusted.

"Does he know that he must die?" I asked of his mother.

"Yes, ma'am, the doctor told him so."

"And how does he feel about it?"

"I don't know, ma'am, only sometimes he clasps his hands together, and looks up and moves his lips, and to-day he tried to sing; and when I put my ear down I heard something about 'wanting to be an angel.' I asked him where he learned it, and he said 'At the workhouse.'"

I put my mouth down to his dull ear, and said, "Do you know who Jesus is, Dick?"

He nodded with his eyes shut, and whispered, "The minister told me, ma'am."

"And do you believe He loves you, Dick?"

One or two tears oozed slowly between the closed lids, and that was all the answer.

"Pray to Him, Dick, as you lie there; just think

your thoughts to Him, and ask him to forgive all you have done that is wrong, and to take you to live with Him in Heaven; and He will do it."

The poor little fellow looked up at me and nodded slowly, and I bade him good-bye.

I went again the next morning, but in the night poor little Dick's fingers had tapped at the heavenly gate, and I believe he was not turned away.

Oh! there are those who walk in white amidst the
    heavenly plains,
Who once, in rags and wretchedness, wandered
    earth's dreary lanes;
Who often vainly begged a crust from the rich
    miser's hoard,
But now, with wedding garments, sit around the
    Father's board;
Who "longed to see the angels" here, and hear
    their heavenly song,
And now in gladness sweep their harps amid the
    shining throng.

SEA-VIEW HOUSE.

By the Editor.

ANNIE THORNTON, and her brother Harry, and her two sisters, Kate and Emma, were all ill at the same time. One day they were all so ill that the doctor said that not one of them might be alive by the end of the week. All that skill and care could do to save their lives was done. God blessed the means that were used, and by the end of the week the children were not only living, but, as the doctor said, in a fair way of doing well. Oh, how glad their papa and mamma, and all their relations and friends were! And how glad the servants were!

At the end of another week the doctor said, " All danger is now over; the children need a cook more than they need a doctor." This was very good news for everybody in the house. The children were so delighted that they begged their mamma to ring the bell at once, send for Cook, and tell her what the doctor said.

"My dears," said mamma, "Cook may be busy now, and I don't like to call her away from her work. When I go down-stairs I can tell her what Dr Wilson says."

"Oh, but, mamma, we should so like to hear what Cook will say—do send for her!"

So Mrs Thornton told the nursemaid to go and tell Cook she was wanted in the nursery.

I think it is very likely that Mary the nursemaid told Cook what she was wanted for; she came back, smiling, to say that Cook would come in a few minutes. The minutes seemed rather long ones— and more than a few.

"What a long time Cook takes to get ready!" said Harry.

"Perhaps she's changing her dress," said Kate.

"Or is in the middle of making a custard," said Emma.

Annie was just about to give *her* opinion, when up came Cook, her shiny red face all over smiles.

The moment the children saw her they said, nearly all together, and in a louder voice than they had spoken for some weeks, "Good morning, Cook!" Harry was then going to tell Cook what the doctor had said, and it may be he was going to order dinner, had not his sisters asked him to "let Mamma tell."

"I'm very glad, ma'am, to see the young ladies, and "——

Cook's speech was cut short by Harry, who exclaimed—

"Yes, Cook, and we're all glad to see you."

But Cook had her speech ready; so, without taking notice of Harry's interruption, she added, "Mr Harry are getting so nicely round."

"Nicely *round!*" cried Annie; "why, we're all skin and bone!"

"Yes, miss, 'xackly so," Cook replied, hardly knowing what to say. But the young folks laughed at Annie's little joke.

Mrs Thornton told Cook what the doctor had said, and added, "I'll have some talk with you about it by and by, Cook."

From the manner in which this was said, and her kind smile, Cook understood Mrs Thornton had said all she wished to say then, and with nods and grins backed out of the room, and was soon heard running down-stairs as if she were afraid that the cat would drink all the new milk before she could get back to her kitchen.

Our young folks had not been used to laughing lately; they were not at all strong, and their laughing made them feel weaker.

Harry was the first to speak.

"There now, mamma," said he, "I was just get-

F

ting breath to tell Cook what we should like, when she ran away as fast as ever she could."

"As though we wanted to eat her!" added Kate.

There was another little laugh, in which mamma joined. Harry's laugh was neither so hearty nor so long. He was quite in earnest about something nice for his dinner.

"It is all very well to make fun," said he; "but what about our dinner?"

"Do have a little patience, my dear boy!" said Mrs Thornton.

"So I have, mamma," was Harry's prompt reply.

And he was quite right. He had a *little* patience —very little indeed; in fact, he could hardly have less, and have any at all. But he meant that he had patience; and like many others, grown-up people as well as children, Harry Thornton could not see himself as others saw him.

Harry was only a few months over nine years of age, but everybody used to say he was "quite a little gentleman."

There is no reason why every boy of nine years of age, and every boy who is old enough to know what is right and what is wrong, and how to behave, should not be "a little gentleman," even though his parents may not be so well off as Harry Thornton's parents were.

I must own that Harry did not always behave as

a gentleman should, and that he seems to have been
called quite a little gentleman as much on account
of his *importance* as on account of his good behaviour, for it is but fair to say that, with all his
faults, few boys of his age behaved better.

You would, I dare say, like to know what I mean
by Harry's *importance.* I will tell you.

He was petted and praised, and "made so much
of," as his nurse says, that he seemed to be one of
the most important persons in Wellington Crescent.

He was not the eldest child, but Miss Thornton
(Annie) was not much more than two years his senior;
and as he was a sharp, clever boy, quick at learning
and clever at all sorts of games in the playroom, his
sisters thought him a perfect wonder.

Harry was on very good terms with himself;
he liked himself quite as much as others liked
him—perhaps a little, just a little more. But he
was not selfish, for all that: if he did not like
everybody quite as well as he liked himself, he
strove to do unto others as he would they should
do unto him.

To his sisters he was as loving and kind as any
brother could be, so it is no wonder that they
"made much of him."

Harry was the only one in the house who had a
bedroom in which no one else slept. It had two

doors, one of which opened into the large room in which his sisters and nurse slept.

When first he slept in it, nurse used to leave the middle door open during the night. His cousin Frank came to see him one day. "Frank! come and see *my* room!" said Harry.

Whenever Harry said "*my* room," he looked at the least an inch taller.

Frank was delighted with Harry's room. He was one of four brothers, of whom he was the youngest but one, and he was not quite as old as Harry.

"Oh, jolly!" said Frank. "Don't I wish I had a room all to myself, and two doors! What's that door for?" and he pointed to the middle door.

"That door? Oh, that's nurse's door; it opens into nurse's room, and it's left open all night."

"Left open all night! Oh! would *I* have one of *my* doors left open all night? Why, it's just like being a baby. I should say, 'Nurse, please be sure to shut both my doors, and I'll ring for you if I want anything.'"

"Well, Frank, I never thought of that," said Harry; "what a good one you are! I'll have a little bell at my bedside, and I'll have both my doors shut."

"Have a bell-rope over your pillow, that's what I should do," said Frank.

"How clever you are, Frank!" cried Harry; "you might grow up to be a conjuror, or a photograph!"

You must know that by "photograph," Harry meant "photographer;" but it was one of the long words which he could not pronounce easily. He had an idea that a conjuror, whom he once saw performing in the street, and the photographer, were the two cleverest men in the world, next to his own papa, of course.

Harry had not much trouble to get his papa to have a bell hung over the head of nurse's bed and a bell-rope over his own; and the very next day after his two doors had been shut all night, Harry wrote a letter to his cousin to tell him that though both doors had been shut all night, he went to sleep and woke up quite well.

I have been saying so much about Harry, that it is time I went on with the tale about the cook.

"Does Cook know what we should like for dinner, mamma?" Harry inquired.

"She will know, very soon, what she is to get ready for you," Mrs Thornton replied.

Harry had not dined with his sisters for more than four weeks. They could not leave their bed, and Harry could not leave his, for more than two weeks; and though it was now a week since the children could be together for a few hours each day in the nursery, they were all too weak to have a meal such as they used to have before they were ill.

The three sisters agreed with Harry that it would be "so nice" to dine together.

Kate said, "You know, dear mamma, we have had no dinner ever since we were ill."

"And no breakfast! And no tea!" said little Emma.

"Poor children! How hungry you must be! I suppose, then, you want Cook to get a very large dinner ready for you. Let me see! how many joints of meat?" said Mrs Thornton.

"Now, mamma, dear, that's your fun. We haven't had a breakfast, or dinner, or tea, like we used to have when we were all well, but we have all had as much as we could eat and drink. We have tried to take the nice things that were brought to us, but we could not."

"Perhaps, though, if we all had dinner together, we should eat more," said Harry.

"Well now, what would you like for your dinner?" mamma asked.

"Let Harry choose for us," said Annie; and her sisters thought that that would be best.

After naming a lot of things that were not in season, or that would be quite unfit for children who were so weak, Harry at last, by mamma's kind help, thought of something that mamma said they might have, and his sisters said he was wonderfully clever to think of what they would all like better than anything else.

The four children were delighted to find how soon their dinner was ready. "Oh! it does look nice, mamma!" said Harry, "but do you think there will be enough for us all? I think I could eat all that myself!"

"And I think I could eat all that, and more too!" said little Emma.

"Well! we shall see how you get on," said Mrs Thornton.

So little was put on each plate, that Harry looked at each of his sisters, then at his plate, and then at each of his sisters again. Had he been as rude as some little boys are, he would have made some remark about it.

Each one looked at the plates in a way that was not quite right, but Emma was the only one to make a remark. She said, " I haven't *too much* on my plate !"

Poor child! she could not eat a quarter of it. Annie and Kate ate very little of theirs, and Harry, who thought that he could eat so much, ate less than either Annie or Kate.

"My dear children," said Mrs Thornton, "now you see what Dr Wilson meant when he said you

want the cook more than the doctor. He meant
that you need food more than you need physic.
You are too weak to eat ; you must have a little as
often as you can take it ; and it must be something
that will do you good. As you get more strength,
you will be able to eat more."

"I think, mamma," said Annie, "if my appetite
were better, I should get stronger."

"You mean," said Harry, "that if you were
stronger, your appetite would be better."

"Annie," said Mrs Thornton, "do you remember
the last sixpence you gave to a poor woman ? "

"Oh yes! mamma ; it was to poor Widow Dawson. She had some needlework to do. Mrs Dash-
ington, when she went out of town, left it to be
sent to her. Widow Dawson could earn money—
I think she said four shillings—by doing the work ;
but she had no needles or cotton, and no money at
all."

"Well, and what then ? "

"Why, mamma, I asked you in a whisper if I
might give her the sixpence I had in my pocket ;
you told me I might, and how pleased Widow
Dawson was that she could buy what she wanted,
and go to work at once ! "

"Well, my dears," said Mrs Thornton, "it is just
the same with strength and appetite. When one
has strength enough to eat a little food, that little

food gives more strength, and that makes the appetite better. So, you see, both Annie and Harry are right."

"What a great appetite Samson must have had, mamma!" said Kate, "for he was so very, very strong!"

Mrs Thornton could not help smiling at this remark of Kate's, and before she had time to make a reply, Harry clapped his poor, thin hands together, and exclaimed—

'Oh! when I get stronger, won't I eat, and eat, and eat, and get stronger, and stronger, and stronger, till at last I may be almost as strong as Samson!"

"My dear boy," said Mrs Thornton, "you must not suppose that those who eat most are the strongest. Those who eat more than is good for them become ill and weak. A little flame will keep a kettle of water boiling a long, long time, but if a kettle of boiling water were kept over a great fire, the water would boil over or go off in steam, till at last the kettle would be empty, and it might even have a hole burnt in it, so that it would not be of use to boil water in again."

"Ah!" said Harry, "I should so like to be strong, so that I could take Kate up and set her on my shoulder, like papa does! But I should like to lie down now, just a little while."

His sisters thought that they would like to lie down too—only for a little while. So the nursery was soon left without anyone in it, and our four young friends were fast asleep.

Harry and his sisters gained strength day by day, but like most children who are getting well, they gave their mamma a world of trouble. They did not mean to be troublesome. No children could love their parents more than they did. But each of them wanted so many things in the course of the day, that their nurse had not much time to sit still. The nursemaid had to go down-stairs so often every day, that when evening came she was as tired as though she had walked many miles, and Mrs Thornton looked so pale, and seemed so weak, that Dr Wilson said she would be quite ill if she did not take more rest.

From the time the children were taken ill, Mrs Thornton had not been out of the house to visit any friends, and very few friends came to No. 57 Wellington Crescent when they heard that there was fever in the house.

The few friends who called did not stay long; and as to going into the nursery—why, they would almost as readily have put their hands into boiling water. "Fever! Oh, how dreadful fever is!" "The four children have fever! Oh, dear! I wouldn't go near the house on any account." In

this way some of the friends of the Thorntons used
to talk.

But Mrs Thornton was not long out of the nursery
the whole time that her children were ill. When
the fever was at its height, she had a bed brought
into the young ladies' bedroom, that she might take
a little rest now and then.

Some nights she would not lie down, even for a
short time. She would not leave her sick children
to the care of the nurse, though the nurse was very
kind. No one, except papa and mamma, nurse, and
the doctor, came into the children's bedrooms.

Nurse was paid double as much for staying in the
house when the children had the fever; and though
she had a great deal to do, she had more time to
rest and to sleep than poor mamma had.

Boys—and girls too—like to read tales about
brave men, they like to hear of bold deeds; but
they too often forget the brave women whom they
know.

Do you, my young friends, know any brave
women ? If you know *mothers*, you are almost
sure to know brave women ; for nearly all mothers,
and all *good* mothers, are brave.

A brave soldier will risk his life for his country.
He thinks less of danger than of the glory of his
country. And what will not a good mother do for
her child ? No brave soldier is more ready to risk

his life in battle than a good mother is to risk her life for her children.

Soldiers are praised by those for whom they fight ; and more than that, they are handsomely rewarded. But how often do children forget how much their mothers have done for them ! No child can ever repay a good mother for all her care. Think of that, my young friends.

Mr Thornton never spent so much time in the nursery as he did when his children were getting well.

One day he came up with an open letter in his hand.

" We are to have a visitor to-day in the nursery," said he.

" A visitor ! " said Mrs Thornton—" who ? "

" Mr Bland."

" Mr Bland ! " exclaimed Annie—" Oh ! I 'm so glad, he 's such a very nice gentleman ! "

" He 's the nicest gentleman I know, next to papa," said Harry.

Kate and Emma were of the same opinion as Annie and Harry.

Mamma, too, seemed quite pleased, and so did papa.

" But papa," said Harry, " will Mr Bland come up into the nursery ? He has never been up here before, has he ? "

" Yes, Harry, he writes to say that his visit

must be a very short one, for he can stay in town only a few hours, but he must come and give each of the convalescents a shake."

"A shake!" cried Kate. "Ah! I know what he means; he wants to shake hands with us."

"And kiss us," said little Emma.

"And make us all laugh," said Annie.

"And tell us lots of tales and all sorts of things, and make up rhymes, and ask us riddles," said Harry. "But, papa, Mr Bland has never been in the nursery before, has he? I don't think he has ever been in *my* room!"

I ought to tell you that the children's bedrooms, and nursery, and play-room, were all on the same floor.

"I don't know," said Mr Thornton, "whether Mr Bland has ever been in this room or in yours, Harry; but I have no doubt that, by the aid of a good map and a guide, he will find his way when he gets as far as the foot of the stairs."

"Oh, papa! you know what Harry means. It would seem so funny to have a gentleman in the nursery."

"Why! I am often here!"

"Yes," said Emma, "but you 're a papa!"

"And Mr Bland is a papa too," said Mr Thornton.

"But he 's not our papa," Emma replied.

"That doesn't matter at all" Harry said, "Mr Bland is a very nice gentleman ; we can all talk to him. Oh! I hope he'll come soon !"

"And stay a good long while !" said Annie.

"I don't know at what time to expect him," said Mr Thornton ; "he may be here very soon, but his stay will be short."

Papa and mamma left the nursery for a short time, and the children found quite enough to talk about. The young ladies, of course, had a little talk about their dresses. Harry told Mary again and again to have his room ready for Mr Bland to see.

I'm sure, Mary, Mr Bland would like to go into *my* room—he has *never in his life* been in *my* room. I was only a little *tinny, tiny* thing, like little Emma, when Mr Bland was here last time, and so I hadn't a room to myself—I wasn't big enough."

As Harry said this, he looked up as if to see if there were any danger of his knocking his head against the ceiling.

Emma did not like to be called "a little *tinny, tiny* thing."

"Harry," said she, "I'm not *tinny, tiny ;* papa says I'm a great girl for my age, and he knows better than you do."

"Why, of course, he does," Harry replied ; "but I shall know what papa knows when I grow up."

Emma did not take any notice of Harry's answer. Her sisters were talking about their dresses, and she cared more to hear what they had to say.

Mamma soon came back, and the nursery was in a few minutes a very busy place.

When all was ready, what wishes there were in the nursery that Mr Bland would come "very, very soon!"

At last Mr Bland came; mamma went downstairs, and how glad was she to hear the merry voices in the nursery!

"He's coming! I heard mamma laugh! Oh! isn't mamma glad he's come!" cried Kate.

"And so is papa glad! And so are we *all* glad!" said Harry.

"And so am *I* glad too!" added Emma.

"Hush!" said Annie, "they're coming up now! We must not make such a noise; Mr Bland will think that we are *so* rude."

The children rose in a quiet proper way when Mr Bland came into the room. He had not been in the nursery long before there was more laughing in it than there had been for a long time.

His visit was very short. Annie said, "Oh, Mr Bland! it doesn't seem that you have been with us five minutes!" when she heard him say that he must go.

"Please write a letter to us, Mr Bland," said Harry.

"And, please, put some rhyme in it," said Annie.

"And some fun," said Emma.

"And a tale," said Kate.

"I will write to you all," said Mr Bland ; "and if I cannot put rhyme, and tales, and fun, all in one letter, I will send you more than one."

The children had enough to talk about after Mr Bland had gone. Almost the first question they asked their mamma was whether she did not think Mr Bland a very nice gentleman—the nicest gentleman of all she knew, except papa ?

"I think I know," said Mrs Thornton, "what you mean by saying Mr Bland is a very nice gentleman ; and I must say I have never seen any gentleman except your own papa who is so great a favourite amongst children."

"And Mr Bland is so wise! Papa says he's very, very clever !" said Harry.

"Yes," Mrs Thornton replied ; "Mr Bland has such a kind heart, and a well-stored mind, and is so pleasing in his manner, that he is much liked by all who know him. There may be many gentlemen as fond of children as Mr Bland is, but they have not the way of talking to them, and pleasing them, that he has."

There was great joy in the nursery the day after

Mr Bland's visit. A letter from Mr Bland! Here
is a copy of it :—

> MY DEAR LITTLE FRIENDS,
> You are now getting well,
> As any one hearing
> Your laughter can tell.
> How glad you must be,
> And how glad are all they
> Who tended you kindly
> By night and by day!
>
> You have often been told
> Of the great God above,
> You have had many proofs
> Of His power and love ;
> And, therefore, dear children,
> As long as you live,
> To God for His mercies
> Your praise you should give.
>
> Try to do what is right,
> And to shun what is wrong,
> And never forget that
> The healthy and strong
> May soon, through an illness,
> Become very weak,
> Not able to stand,
> Scarcely able to speak.

There are some little folks—
  There are grown-up folks too,
Who say God knows all
  That they say and they do ;
And yet they are naughty
  In words and in deeds,
And seem to forget
  That God wickedness heeds.

They think, when they're old,
  Or they lie ill in bed,
They can soon become good ;
  But they very much dread.
To live, whilst they're young,
  Or they're well, as they should,
As " Folks can't be cheerful
  Or laugh if they're good."

Now this is so stupid.
  You may see many folks
Who always seem happy
  And fond of good jokes ;
Who can tell funny stories,
  And join in a game,
Yet who say not nor do
  What is worthy of blame.

Well, try to be like them ;
"Be merry and wise,"
And never be idle—
Time speedily flies ;
Attend to your lessons,
Be active in play,
And try to grow wiser
And better each day.

Now, I think I have written rhyme enough for this time. I began the letter in rhyme, because Annie asked for rhyme, and she is the eldest. All the rhyme is "out of my own head" except "Be merry and wise." Some one else said that a long, long time ago.

It is Emma's turn next—for she spoke next—and she is the youngest old lady in the nursery. She wants fun. I wish you had all been with me in the omnibus in which I rode from Wellington Crescent to the railway station yesterday. How you would have laughed! A very stout old lady —ever so much older and bigger than Emma—got into the omnibus. She was old enough and big enough to be grandmother to a dozen or more old ladies like Emma. She had a very red face, and a very big black bonnet with yellow strings, and roses inside almost as big as young red cabbages. In one hand she had a large cotton umbrella; it had no band to it; and it opened wide as she was getting into the omnibus. The old lady found it no easy matter to close her umbrella before she took her seat. On her left arm she had a large basket, with a lid on each side of the handle.

The poor old lady was quite out of breath, she had walked so fast to catch the omnibus.

She had not sat down long before a strange sound was heard in the omnibus—

"*Me-ow! Me-ow!! Mee-ow!!!*" Just then the omnibus was stopped, and a gentleman with a bag in his hand got out. As he passed the old lady, there was another loud "*Me-ow!*" which made him turn round; and somehow he managed to make the old lady's umbrella open and tumble against the basket, which she had put on the vacant seat beside her. The gentleman was very sorry—very, but he was in a hurry, so he got out of the omnibus as quickly as he could.

"Right!" shouted the conductor, as with a bang he shut the door. And on went the omnibus.

"He didn't let the cat out of the bag," said a gentleman to a lady who was sitting next to him.

"Do you think it was he who had the cat?" the lady asked.

"I do," said the gentleman.

The old lady had put her basket on the seat again by this time, and had tied a piece of string round the umbrella, nearly at the top, to keep it from falling open again.

The omnibus had not gone far when, from under the old lady's dress, or from under her seat came the sound—

"*Me-ow! Mee-ow!!*"

"Oh! it's a kittie!" said a little girl, about as big as Kate—Kate is a great girl, as everybody knows.

"Ugh! I hate cats!" said a cross-looking old gentleman.

"I think it is only a kitten," said a lady, who looked and spoke just like a mamma.

"So much the worse, ma'am. I hope the brute won't come near me! I hate cats! Ugh! where is it?"

Everybody began to look about.

"It's only a little cat," said the big old lady; "it's only a little cat, *a'most a kitten, that won't hurt nobody.* Poor Pussie!" and the old lady gently raised one of the lids of the basket. Just as she did so, she screamed "Oh dear!"

"Scratched her!" said the cross-looking old gentleman; "and serve her right!"

"No, nor it hasn't scratched her neither!" said the old lady, looking very angry; "if you had a cat and kittens of your own, sir, you'd know better than to talk like that."

"*Me-ow! Mee-ow!!*"

"Oh! it's under the seat," said the old lady. Up she got, and down went her umbrella, the handle of it giving the knuckles of the old gentleman such a sharp crack, that he shook his hand in such a way that everyone in the omnibus laughed, except the old lady. Now I come to think of it, it was rude to laugh, but who could help it?

But where was Pussie? Not under the old lady's seat; everyone in the omnibus, except the old gentleman, helped the old lady to look for Pussie, which she said was a *purty critter* (she meant a *pretty* creature), that Mrs Boggles or Mrs Goggles, or some one with a fine name of that kind, had given her for her married daughter, who was *invested* with mice (she meant whose house was *infested* with mice).

The old gentleman would not move, nor help to look for Pussie.

"Are you going as far as the station?" asked a gentleman who sat near to the old lady—it was the same one who spoke of letting the cat out of the bag.

"Yes, sir, I be," said the old lady; "but deary, deary me, what am I to do about that *purty critter?* If she gets out first and runs away, why, what's to become of her? She's quite strange about this here part, you see, sir, and isn't like one of us as can ask the way."

"Now, you sit still," said the gentleman ; "make yourself quite easy about Pussie. I'll take care she doesn't run away—she's safe enough."

"Thank you kindly, sir," said the old lady.

"*Me-ow!*"

"Ah, I hear her—the *purty critter!*" said the old lady.

"Kittie! kittie! kittie!" said the little girl.

"*Me-ow! Me-ow!*"

"Where *can* the *purty critter* be?" cried the old lady, turning sharply round, and letting her big umbrella fall on the feet of the cross old gentleman. He may have had corns. He was so angry that I think he had. We all tried not to laugh, not even to smile, but we all had a little *cough* about the same time ; and the old gentleman said, or rather *growled,* something about "old women and cats," that made us all laugh outright.

The old lady looked more vexed than sorry.

"*Me-ow! Mee-ow!!*"

"*Purty critter!*" said the old lady.

"*Ugh!*" growled the old gentleman.

In a whisper, loud enough for every one to hear, the gentleman who promised to look after Pussie, said to the lady, who sat next to him—

"I think it's under his seat."

(The old gentleman made another growling noise. His "Ugh!" meant a good deal, I daresay.)

"Do you think so?" the lady asked.

"Why, where else can it be? We have looked everywhere else," said the young gentleman.

"Ugh! Hi! Stop! I'll get out here," said the cross old gentleman.

As he rose from his seat, the gentleman who was to take care that Pussie did not run away looked under the seat. Pussie was not there. The old gentleman was out of the omnibus, but where was Pussie? "Feel in your pocket, sir," the young gentleman said to the old one.

Now the old gentleman had such great pockets that a large kitten might easily have got into one of them as he sat in the omnibus; and two of his pockets looked bulky enough for him to have had a cat and a lot of kittens in each.

But the idea of his having a cat in his pocket made him so angry that, instead of feeling his pockets, he walked away as fast as he could.

"Right!" shouted the conductor, as he shut the door with a bang, and on the omnibus rattled over the stones, making such a noise that the gentleman could not hear a word that the old lady was saying to him, and as we were so close to the railway station, he just kept nodding his head as if to say "yes" to all the old lady said.

We reached the station. The gentleman got out first, to see that Pussie did not run away.

"Stop, sir!" the old lady shouted, "didn't you say you would give that man in charge, and we should be sure to find him here?"

"No, my good woman, you make a mistake. I never thought of such a thing."

"Oh, my *purty, purty critter!* to be run off with! and with such a man as that!"

Poor woman! we were sorry for her, but we could not help smiling. The gentleman said "The cat must be somewhere in the omnibus. You stay in till everyone else is out. I'll see that the cat doesn't run away."

"Thank you kindly, sir—the *purty, purty critter!* and my Polly so *invested!*"

As I had a few minutes to spare, I waited to see the "purty critter"—if she could be found. The others in the omnibus were also interested in Pussie, and stood round the door of the omnibus in which was the old lady in search of her *purty critter.*

"One fool makes many," and a few gazers will soon gather a crowd in a large town.

A dirty ragged little boy shouted out, "Hi! Bill! come on! 'ere's a haxident!"

"An accident!" shouted a shopman, who had brought a parcel to the station.

"What's the matter?" asked one. "Anyone hurt?" asked another. All sorts of questions were asked, and all sorts of persons were round the omnibus.

And what was to be seen ? An old lady very red in the face, and very angry, in an omnibus. And what was to be heard ?—only this, the old lady calling out—" The bad, *bad* man to run off with my *purty critter !*—my *purty critter !* "

" Has she lost her daughter?" asked a butcher-boy of a newspaper-boy.

" No ! Only her cat."

" Now, missis, please, you see there's ne'er a cat in the 'bus—come along ! " cried the conductor.

The old lady put her empty basket on her arm and went to the corner of the omnibus for her umbrella. As she came to the door there was a shout of laughter, that, in less time than it takes me to write these words, brought quite a crowd of persons.

Through a hole in the large umbrella was poked the head of a pretty tabby kitten ! The kitten was looking about her as though there was fine fun going on.

You see, when the gentleman who first got out of the omnibus, threw down the old lady's umbrella and basket, he let the kitten out of the basket, though he did not let the cat out of the bag ; the kitten ran into the big umbrella, and then she had no way of getting out again ; but by a little patience, and biting, and scratching, she had made a small hole, large enough to get her little head through, just to see what was going on.

I was glad that the old lady found her *purty critter.* I had seen so much fun. I hope that Kate will take the tale of the kitten (not the kitten's *tail*) as the tale she wanted me to send her; and as she didn't ask for *fun*, all the fun is for Emma, who is so loving to her sisters and brother, that I daresay she will allow them to have a few smiles.

Harry only wanted a letter, so he is sure to be satisfied, for this is a very long one. I did go into his room, as I promised I would. If I were a boy now, I should like to be Harry Thornton, with such good, kind parents and three such dear, loving sisters, and a bedroom and *bell-rope* all to himself, and all his wants so well supplied.

The young convalescent of Wellington Crescent ought to be as happy as a little prince. There was once an English prince called " Madcap Harry ; " but he was not the son of Mr and Mrs Thornton, and his sisters were not Annie, Emma, and Kate. Ask papa or mamma to tell you about " Madcap Harry."

I must now, once more, say good-b'ye to you all, and I will try to write another letter to you next week. Believe me, your affectionate friend,

URBAN BLAND."

Mr Bland's letter gave much pleasure to the young folks. But I think that the next letter they had from him pleased them still more.

As he lived in a very pleasant town on the sea coast, Mr Thornton asked him to be kind enough to look out for a nice house for him.   He wanted, as the fine warm weather was coming, to take his family to the sea-side for a month or six weeks.

Mr Bland could not see a house that would suit Mr Thornton, but Mrs Bland thought of a very good plan, and a very kind one too.   She said to Mr Bland, " As we are going to Paris for a month, and don't want to let our house here to strangers, why not invite Mr and Mrs Thornton to come with their family to take charge of the house for us ?   We may as well stay six weeks in Paris as a month."

Mr and Mrs Thornton were very glad of the kind offer, and so were the children, who thought it would be so nice to be such a long time in Mr Bland's house.

" I think," said Harry, " it would be nicer still if we could all go to Mr Bland's by the sea-side, and he and Mrs Bland, and William, and Edward, and Maria, and Alice, and Bessie," (these were the names of Mr Bland's children) " were to stay at home."

" But, my dear boy," said Mrs Thornton, " the house would not be large enough for two families ; indeed, the only fault that Mr Bland has to find with his house is that it is scarcely large enough,"

" I hope Mr Bland will write to us when he is in Paris," said Annie.

"Well, Annie, you had better write to him and ask him."

"And write for me as well, please, Annie," said Emma.

"I'll write to ask him as well," said Harry; "shall I write for you, Kate?"

"How kind you are, Harry. Yes, do, please. I don't much like writing letters; my pen always turns bad, and then I make mistakes."

"All the fault of the pen!" said Harry, laughing.

"No, not all, perhaps; but—well, never mind. You write for me, there's a dear good boy."

So Annie and Harry each wrote a very nice letter, to which Mr Bland replied, promising to write, at the least, once a-week all the time he was in Paris; but he should expect, at the least, one letter a-week from his young friends in return.

Mr Bland's letters to Harry Thornton and his sisters would make quite a little book; and perhaps some day you will read them in a little book.

But I must tell you what Mr Bland wrote to Harry about his bedroom. He wrote that, as William and Edward would sleep in Paris, they would not be able to sleep at the same time in their room at Sea-view House in Sussex, and that they would be very glad if their friend, Harry Thornton, would take care of it for them. In his letter, Mr Bland wrote, "as the bedroom and the

bed are large enough for two, I do hope that it
will be large enough for you. The room has two
doors, like your room in Wellington Crescent ; the
middle door opens into the room in which the young
ladies sleep, so that you will soon find yourself
quite at home. As I know you like a bell-rope, I
have had one hung over your pillow."

"Oh! isn't he good?" cried Harry. "Now,
that's what I call a gentleman—bell-rope and all!"

"But, Harry," said Annie, "you never used your
bell-rope till you were ill. You promised papa that
you would not pull it if there was no *great need*
for some one to come to you at once. You rang
the bell often enough the week before the doctor
said we might get up."

"Yes, and since then, too!" said Kate. "Wasn't
it funny of Mr Bland to say, that if Harry were so
fond of ringing a bell, he should be a muffin-boy ?"

"Oh! but he didn't mean that, I know well
enough," said Harry. "Would he ask a muffin-boy
anything about Latin."

"About Latin ? " cried Kate.

"Yes, he asked me how I was getting on with
my *hic musa ;* and what's the muse to do with
muffins, I should like to know ?"

"I'm sure I can't tell you," said Kate.

"Neither can I," said Emma. "Ask Annie."

Emma looked so earnest when she said this, that

Annie, and Harry, and Kate, could not help laughing.

"A bell-rope! oh!" said Harry, as closing his two hands, he gave them a jerk as though he were grasping the rope of a very heavy bell.

"Oh! a bell-rope all to myself in *my* room, and I haven't had to promise not to pull *that* bell-rope. Oh! stay till I get to my room in Sea-view House!"

. . . . .

The long-wished-for day came at last, and after a very pleasant railway ride, Harry and his sisters were, with papa and mamma, in Sea-view House, and to the surprise of our young friends a nice dinner was ready for them.

And they were soon ready to dine. How they enjoyed their dinner! Harry's appetite was better than it had been since his illness.

"Mamma, dear," said Mr Thornton, "you will not feel disposed to go for a walk this evening; neither shall I ; so if you will try the piano, I shall be very glad of a little music."

"Papa, please, may I *try the bell?*" said Harry.

"Try the bell! Harry! what do you mean, my son ?"

"Why, sir, I mean *my* bell—my *bell-rope*—in *my* room."

"Oh! by all means."

Harry was delighted, and though it was a great

treat for him and for his three sisters to dine with papa and mamma, he was not sorry when dinner was over.

"Let us all go and see *my* room," said Harry, as soon as he thought he might do so.

" Do you want us *all* to *try the bell*, Harry ?" Mr Thornton asked.

" I can pull for everyone," said Harry ; " but if anyone else *wants* to try *my* bell-rope "——

" No, no, Harry ; you shall pull for us all," said Mr Thornton.

Harry's room was soon found, and he was much pleased with it.

"What's that string for, papa ?" said Harry, pointing to a string which stretched from the top of a large box at the side of the bed to the top of the bell-rope."

" I really don't know ; but you had better not meddle with it," Mr Thornton said. "Now for your merry peal !"

With both hands, Harry took hold of the bell-rope.

" Now, be steady, Harry," mamma said, " or you may break the wire."

Henry pulled, but instead of hearing a bell ring, a dull, heavy sound was heard at the bedside.

" What's that ?" cried Harry. "What's that ?" cried several voices, and all eyes were turned towards the big box. The lid was thrown back as Harry pulled the bell-rope.

" You see the use of that string now, Harry," said Mr Thornton ; " it is to open the box."

" What a strange way to open the box!" said Kate.

" What 's the box for ? " said Annie, and the three girls made a rush towards it.

" Oh ! " cried one ; " Oh, look ! " cried another ; " Oh, how beautiful ! " cried a third one. The box was full of all sorts of toys. Right at the top was a large wax doll nicely dressed, and on the doll was a letter addressed to " Miss Thornton, of No. 57 Wellington Crescent." .

" This letter is for you, Annie, dear," said Mrs Thornton. " It is, I see, from Mr Bland."

Annie opened the letter and read as follows :—

" MY DEAR ANNIE,—All the toys in the box are for you and Harry and your sisters ; I know that Harry will be sure to open the box as soon as he gets into his room. I promised that he should have a bell-rope all to himself, and he has it. Tell him that some day he shall have a bell, and muffins. All here send best love to you all there. Your affectionate friend,   URBAN BLAND."

Just as Annie had finished reading the letter, there was a gentle tap at the door. " Come in,"

H

said Mrs Thornton. It was a servant. "Please, ma'am, the bell-hanger was to come at six o'clock; he's down-stairs, ma'am—Mr Bland ordered him to hang a bell for the young gentleman."

"There now!" said Harry. "Oh, we are happy!"

His sisters all agreed with him in that, and so did his parents.

The time seemed to pass so happily, that our young friends said they didn't think they could be so happy.

One day when they were sitting very happily talking about the many blessings they had, papa said, "My dear children, we should strive to show our thankfulness by deeds as well as by words. Our kind friend Mr Bland will not hear of my paying him anything for our living in this nice house of his. He is a good man and very thoughtful. He says if I have any money to spare, he will be glad if I will give it to the Hospital for Sick Children."

"What is that, papa?" Annie asked.

"It is a large house in which the sick children of very poor people are taken care of; they have doctors and nurses, just as though their parents were well off; they have nice food, and all they want. But all that costs money; furniture, and coals, and food must be paid for; nurses must be paid. And where is the money to come from?

I could not pay it all, neither could Mr Bland. But if Mr Bland and I, and a good many more, give as much as we can afford, there will be money enough to soothe the pain, and perhaps save the lives of many, many poor little children."

"I would give something to the Hospital if I could," said Annie.

Harry, Kate, and Emma said the same thing in nearly the same words.

"My dear children," Mrs Thornton said, "you can all do something, even if it be but little. A penny will buy an orange or a toy for a poor little convalescent."

"Oh, mamma! don't you think that we four, who might have died if papa had been too poor to buy all that was wanted for us when we were so ill, ought to do something for poor children who are ill?" Kate asked.

"I do indeed," was Mrs Thornton's reply.

"And we will!" said Henry.

"And we will!" said each of the girls.

"My dear children," said Mr Thornton, "I am glad to hear you speak so, and I hope and trust that you will never forget your promise. Whenever you hear of children of poor people being ill, think of God's great goodness to you—you cannot think of *all* His goodness to you, but you *can* think of SEA-VIEW HOUSE."

MISS MUFF AND LITTLE HUNGRY.

PART I.

I MUST tell you a tale about money,
    And two little girls who had none ;
Although it's an every-day story—
No novelty under the sun.

The first one—I think you must know her,
    She lives, very likely, next door ;
And the second—you've certainly met her
    A hundred times, maybe, or more.

But listen, and see if you know them
    As well as they ought to be known ;
And if any one part of my story
    Sounds just like a part of your own.

Miss Muff once went out for an airing,
    On a bitter cold winter day,
And many a one smiled to her,
    As she carried her dolly so gay.

Her face was so round and so rosy,
    People said, as they pass'd one by one,
" Why, she looks like a dear little bundle!
    A bundle of comfort and fun!"

For her frock was of finest merino,
    Her boots were as warm as could be;
And two little blanket-like leggings
    Wrapp'd round from the foot to the knee.

The bonnet was silk, neatly quilted;
    The cloak was well wadded all through;
Round her neck hung a furry gray tippet,
    And each wrist had its furry cuff too.

Even dolly was dress'd in the warmest,
    And muffled in cloth and in silk;
With her cheeks that were red as spring tulips,
    And her forehead as white as new milk.

And there she seemed laughing and dancing
    In the funniest sort of a way;
While Muff held her little kid fingers,
    For fear she should dance quite away.

They stopp'd and look'd in at the windows
    Where other dolls hung in a row;
With woolly dogs, waggons, and kitchens,
    Gray kittens, and cocks that would crow.

They went into shops to buy candy,
　And they went into shops just for play;
And there was not a happier couple
　Than Muff and her dolly that day.

There stood upon one of those corners,
　Where the winter winds played hide-and-seek,
A child who seem'd waiting for courage,
　Or waiting for power to speak.

Her face was so thin and so frozen,
　Her lips were so blue with the cold,
That, whatever her pitiful story,
　It seem'd it could hardly be told.

Sometimes, as the ladies swept by her,
　She held out one little stiff hand,
And pleadingly look'd in their faces—
　For surely they *must* understand.

And then as they pass'd her, unheeding,
　And floated away, gay and sweet,
She patiently waited—and shiver'd—
　And look'd up and look'd down the street.

But when she saw Muff and her dolly,
　Her deep-sunk hunger-worn eyes
Could not leave her again for a moment,
　And even grew bright with surprise.

And Muff, every bit as astonish'd,
 Stopp'd short where she was in the street,
And stood there and gazed at the beggar—
 Her rags, and her bare hands and feet.

And while other people strode onward,
 And the wind whistled carelessly by,
Muff listen'd, and heard little Hungry
 Break forth with her pitiful cry—

" A penny !—please, ma'am, a penny !
 Sweet lady, just give me one!
All day I have not had any,
 And the day is nearly done.

" My basket, you see, is empty,
 And my feet are all aching with cold ;
If I was not so very hungry,
 I never should be so bold."

" Little girl, why do you go ragged,
 And stand in the street to beg ?
And why don't you have a stocking
 To cover your little bare leg ? "

" O lady, we have no money,
 And very little to eat ;
And mother says, if we must starve
 We may as well starve in the street.

" And maybe some blessed lady,
  Or gentleman, kind and good,
Might pity the poor little beggar—
  My mother said, maybe they would.

" So, lady, please give me a penny,
  Dear lady, to buy some bread !
For mother can't work as she used to,
  And father has long been dead."

" Little girl, I would give you a penny ;
  Mamma gave me four shillings to-day ;
But the things that I like are so many,
  I 've spent all my money away.

" I wanted a hat for my dolly,
  And those little red shoes for her feet ;
And by that time, you know, we were hungry,
  And had to get something to eat.

" And then, after all, I ate nothing
  But two little pieces of cake ;
For the icing that cover'd the last one
  Made this little wicked tooth ache.

" So, poor little girl, I have nothing ;
  My very last shilling I spent ;
If I had any left you should have it."
  Then onward she smilingly went.

PART II.

Miss Muff went home to her dinner,
   And fail'd not to tell to her nurse
What she 'd seen,—the events of the morning,
   And how she had emptied her purse.

She took off her cuffs and her tippet,
   And tumbled them down on the bed,
And carefully lifted the bonnet
   That cover'd her gay little head.

Still all the time talking and laughing,
   And telling the sights she had seen ;
The poor little girl at the corner,
   And the lady in purple and green.

" Dear, dear ! " said the nurse, " who 'd have
      thought it !
   That you should stand still in the street,
A-talking to all the young beggars
   That ever you happen to meet.

" Why some day you 'll freeze all your fingers,
   And maybe the half of your toes ;
And like as not catch from the beggars
   Some terrible illness—who knows ?

"But run down to the parlour, my pigeon,
  Mamma is just waiting for you;
I know who'll have turkey for dinner,
  And custard and apple-pie too."

Miss Muff went down to the parlour,
  And gave her mamma a good hug;
And then she stood still by the fire,
  Her feet on the soft velvet rug.

The fire went blazing and crackling,
  And Muff warm'd each fat little hand,
And thought about beggars and candy,
  Things wiser heads don't understand.

"Mamma," she said gravely, "when people
  Have nothing to wear or to eat,
Why do you suppose they like better
  To come out and die on the street?"

"My dear," said her mother, "what nonsense!
  Why, what makes you talk of such things?
But what has become of our dinner?
  Muff, give the bell two or three rings."

Miss Muff rang the bell, and the servant
  Flung open the dining-room door;
And the room seem'd to glitter with comfort
  As it never had glitter'd before.

The firelight danced up the chimney,
  And the gaslights burn'd clear overhead ;
And the dinner for two that was spread there
  Was enough for a dozen instead.

There was cranberry sauce for the turkey,
  And potatoes both golden and white ;
With celery, cold ham, and oysters,
  And more, that I won't stop to write.

You 'd hardly have thought it was winter,
  The room was so cheerful and warm ;
Within all was shining with comfort,
  But without was a wild winter storm.

So gravely Miss Muff ate her turkey,
  And gravely took pieces of bread ;
She scarcely could relish her dinner,
  With so many thoughts in her head.

She heard the wind roar in the chimney,
  And knew how it blew in the street ;
The sharp icy hail was beginning
  On window and pavement to beat.

She look'd at the gay crackling fire,
  And mamma's dress, of rich silken stuff ;
And thought of that poor empty basket,
  And her plate—where was more than enough

Then tasted the pie and the custards,
   And wonder'd, and wonder'd, and thought;
Till the waiter again clear'd the table,
   And the almonds and raisins were brought.

"Mamma, why don't people get money,
   And not be so dreadfully poor,
And buy themselves bonnets and tippets?
   It would be a good plan, I am sure."

"Indeed," said Mamma, "I can't tell you,—
   Just hand me a nut-cracker, dear;—
But if people will choose to be wicked,
   Why then they must suffer, I fear."

"Oh, are all the poor people wicked?"
   Said Muff, with her wide-open eyes;
"Mamma, would my poor little beggar
   Be better for turkey and pies?"

"And pray, who is your little beggar?
   And where have you been all the day?
And could you find nothing more pleasant
   Than beggars to see in your way?"

"Yes, mamma, I saw plenty of people,
   Dressed out just as fine as could be;
Would such clothes make my child a good beggar?
   I should like to try *that*—just to see!"

"What nonsense you talk!" said her mother,—
"As foolish as foolish can be.
Go read your new story-books, darling,
Or play with your dolly till tea.

"These beggars you talk of are naughty;
They're children for whom no one cares;
They won't wash their clothes or their faces,
And I daresay not one says her prayers."

"And then, were they pretty and cleaner,
And had ribbons, and dresses, and lace, .
And said their prayers too, God would love them,"
Said Muff, with her serious face.

"Why, yes—I don't know—I suppose so;
Dear me, what strange things children say!
You can talk of such things when you're older,—
Now, darling, run off to your play."

Muff went and sat down on the hearth-rug,
And tried on her dolly's new hat;
But for waiting till she was much older,
Her thoughts would not hear about that.

PART III.

Little Hungry had crept round the corner,
  And trotted away down the street,
In one little summer-thin garment,
  And with two little icy-cold feet.

Then seated herself on a door-step,
  And open'd her basket and store,
And brought out two crusts, dry and mouldy ;
  Little Hungry could find nothing more.

So mouldy, you would not have touch'd them;
  So dry, it was all she could do,
Though her teeth were well sharpen'd with hunger,
  To bite the hard bits through and through.

And there she sat munching her dinner,
  With plentiful tables so nigh ;
Fresh loaves in plain sight at the baker's,
  And the smell of roast beef floating by.

On her head God's sweet sunshine lay lightly,
  Streaming on her from heaven's own door ;
But no human smile came to cheer her,—
  People look'd, and pass'd on,—nothing more.

The lady in green and in purple
  Trail'd along her magnificent dress ;
She was loaded with all sorts of blessings,
  But she never attempted to bless.

The gentleman clothed so warmly
  Never stopp'd by the way to inquire
If the beggar-child lived in a cellar,
  And if she had food and a fire.

People look'd, and said, " Oh, how distressing
  To see such a sight in the street !
To see a child eating her dinner
  With fingers as black as her feet !

"Did one ever imagine such tatters ?
  Or see such a hat on a head ?—
And it is only just fit to hold cinders,
  That basket she has for her bread."

So they drew to the edge of the pavement,
  And kept as far off as they could ;
So busy in thinking " you should not,"
  That they never remember'd " *I should.*"

The wind gaily play'd with their feathers,
  And stroked their soft tippets of fur ;
Then gave little Hungry a shiver,—
  It had nothing but roughness for her.

Their rich silken robes swept the pavement,
  And caught that same dust from the street
Which, to their disgust and annoyance,
  Had cover'd her poor little feet.

But who could see dust on such dresses?
  And what could such ladies do wrong?
The very air seem'd to grow sweeter
  For them as they flutter'd along.

Flutter'd home to their well-furnish'd houses,
  Their fires, and dinners, and rest;
Where all they could look at and handle
  Was made of the richest and best.

Miss Muff lived in one of these houses,
  And her intimate friend lived next door;
And below, and above, and just near her,
  You could count up such friends by the score.

But who shall describe the dark alley—
  The one little Hungry dwelt in?
That byeway of dirt and of sorrow,
  Of poverty, suffering, and sin?

Who shall tell how the many were crowded
  In places too small for a few;
How, while some got a living by thieving,
  Others starved—having nothing to do.

I

The place with its great heaps of rubbish—
 Ashes, cabbage-leaves, old bones, and rags ;
Which the rag-pickers search'd every morning,
 Putting many a scrap in their bags.

The houses, all ruin'd and dirty ;
 The men, with their dark lives of crime ;
The children—more dirty, more ruin'd—
 The women, that fought half the time.

Who shall tell of the air that was breathed there ?
 Who shall speak of the sights that were seen,
So very few streets from the dwelling
 Of the lady in purple and green !

Within a stone's throw of the mansions
 Where gay dinner-tables were set
For the gentlemen wrapp'd up in broadcloth
 Who had this poor alley to let ?

Yes, *they* own'd the tumble-down houses ;
 They let all those cellars for gold ;
They knew how the small rooms were crowded
 With poverty, hunger, and cold.

They knew how the sharp broken pavement
 Was trodden by wretched bare feet ;
They knew that the city street-cleaners
 Were never sent into *that* street.

But the alley was left in its foulness,
    And the people lived on as they might,
In darkness, and evil, and suffering,
    With twenty church steeples in sight.

And there little Hungry crept homeward,
    Found nothing to eat, as she said;
Then took a few blows for her supper, .
    And lay on the floor for a bed.

So the winter day came to its ending,
    And Darkness and Night ventured out;
All over and through the great city
    They went silently, swiftly about.

In a robe gaily spangled with gas-lights
    Night walk'd at her ease, bright as day,
And watch'd by the well-furnish'd houses,
    Lest some one by chance went astray.

But Darkness, all muffled and gloomy,
    Join'd hands with the wind and the sleet,
And down on the close narrow alleys,
    Where the poor people lived, took her seat,

What matter if *they* slipp'd and stumbled?
    Their rags wouldn't spoil in the storm;
And all the brocade in the city
    Was safe, and the broadcloth was warm.

PART IV.

Another day came in its brightness,
   When the world look'd all glad as before ;
And Muff gaily tripp'd down the staircase,
   And open'd the heavy street-door.

Then turn'd down the very next crossing,
   And march'd off the very same way ;
And eagerly look'd for her beggar,—
   For Muff had a great deal to say.

And presently where the green ivy
   Climbs lovingly up the church wall,
Where the church-goers weekly come thronging
   When the bell sounds its musical call;

She found little Hungry—just standing,
   Her face on the iron rails press'd ;
And her fingers thrust through, vainly striving
   To pull one green leaf from the rest.

One leaf !—and was that all her portion ?
   One leaf from the cold outside wall,
When leaves for the healing of nations
   Were within, offer'd freely to all !

Now Muff was not learnèd in lectures,
    Nor knew much of giving advice;
So the minute she saw little Hungry
    She pour'd out her thoughts in a trice.

" Little girl, it's because you are naughty
    That you have so little to eat;
If you were a good little beggar,
    You never need stay in the street.

" But people must wash their own faces,
    And brush out their hair a great deal,
And make themselves neat little children,
    No matter how badly they feel.

" So Mamma says, when I say I'm tired,
    And call it a bother to dress;
And Nurse says it's folks that look pretty
    That God up in heaven will bless.

" And then you must always remember
    To say your prayers twice every day
You can ask for just what you wish for,—
    God hears every word that you say "

Little Hungry had listen'd and wonder'd
    With a face that said, " Is it all true? "
And when Miss Muff spoke about praying,
    Her thin blue lips utter'd, " Do you? "

"Why, yes !" said Miss Muff; "what a question !
   To be sure I do, morning and night;
When I'm ready to come down to breakfast,
   And before Nurse has put out the light.

"There are so many things that might happen
   When we are alone in the dark,
And all the day long we want something,
   As I've heard Mamma often remark.

"So you must kneel down on the hearth-rug,
   And say your prayers nicely and slow,
And ask God to keep you and bless you,—
   It'll make you feel better, you know."

" I don't know any prayers," said the beggar,
   Looking up with her pitiful eyes ;
"You see, I live down in the alley,
   And God's away up in the skies."

"But God can look down in the alley,
   And hear just as well," said Miss Muff;
" And I only say just ' Our Father,'
   And ' For Jesus' sake,'—that's quite enough."

Miss Muff turn'd away with her dolly,
   And the sunshine dropp'd down in the west ;
And everything bright on the pathway
   Hurried on to its home and its rest.

And down to the dark noisy alley
  Little Hungry crept back for the night,
Looking up to those far, far blue heavens,
  All aglow with the pink evening light.

" But they make such a noise in our alley,
  I don't think God ever can hear ;
And then it's so dirty and ugly,
  He never would come very near.

" And then if He lives up in heaven,
  He couldn't care much about me ;
The rich people push me and scold me,—
  And why God shouldn't too, I don't see."

But still as she trotted on sadly,
  Her little heart gave its low cry :
" Our Father !   For Jesus' sake, hear me ! "
  And still she look'd up to the sky.

And down from the sky God was looking,
  Right into that poor little face,
With His eyes, which see   straight through the
    darkness,
  And His love, which can warm every place.

People push'd her aside, and said, " Really,
  These beggars are under one's feet ! "
And God saw the beggar, and touched her
  With pity so tender and sweet.

He sent such a message of comfort,
    He gave such a thought of His love,
'Twas as if that warm flush of the evening
    Had dropp'd in her heart from above.

And in spite of the dark, noisy alley,
    In spite of the dull, aching head,
Though without any fire or supper,
    Little Hungry went happy to bed.

She did not kneel down on the hearth-rug;
    No carpet nor hearth-rug was there;
The boards were all dirty and broken
    Where *she* knelt to say her short prayer.

But the words went as straight up to heaven,
    And God was as ready to hear,
And the little child wearily rested,
    For Jesus seem'd there, very near.

Though she was a poor little beggar,
    So ragged, so helpless, so small;
Yet Jesus remember'd and loved her,
    And Jesus is King over all.

She crept to her place in the corner,
    And lay on the hard wooden floor,
Where the wind stirr'd her hair and her tatters,
    Roaming in through the old broken door,

Then thought of her Father in heaven,
  " Our Father "—the words came so sweet!
Then breathed out the dear name of Jesus,
  And fell fast asleep at His feet!

PART V.

.When the King shall come in His glory,
  With bright angels thronging around,
And before Him are gather'd all nations
  At the summoning trumpet's sound;

When He comes in the clouds of heaven,
  And sits on His great white throne;
Who, among the countless millions,
  Will the great King of glory then own?

Who shall have His blest word of approval,
  Be welcomed, and joyfully stand,
White-robed and crowned with honour,
  The blessèd, at His right hand?

On whom will He look with favour?
  To whom will He say " Well done!"
When the days of service are ended,
  And the day of judgment begun?

Will it be the rich ones only?
  Or will it be only the great?
At the King's right hand in glory
  Are those who have learned to wait.

The flush of eternal daylight
  Will dawn on many a brow,
That is wrapp'd in earthly shadows,
  And heavy with darkness now.

Will it be the strong and the happy,
  Who never knew want or care?
Oh, many a life-long prisoner
  Stands free in the heavenly air!

There 'll be many a bow'd head lifted,
  And many a sore heart heal'd,
In the day when all souls are gather'd,
  And the secrets of all reveal'd.

Will it be the well and the hearty,
  Who never have felt a pain?
Look up to the right hand of Jesus,
  Where loss is for ever made gain!

There are eyes that saw first heaven's glory,
  And ears that heard nought till its song;
Glad feet on the bright golden pavement,
  That halted in this mortal throng.

There are poor, with unfading riches,
   And despised that are wearing a crown,
And unknown and unheard-of strangers,
   To whom the Lord giveth renown.

The followers of the Lord Jesus,
   Of every name and hue ;
Not those who were wise and learned,
   But those who were faithful and true ;

Who honour'd Him in the fire,
   Who follow'd Him through the wave,
And, living or dying, look'd only
   To Him who was mighty to save.

The King will divide the people,
   And these shall stand on His right
In the blaze of heaven's glory,
   And those on His left in night.

And then shall He say : " Ye blessed,
   Come into the joy of your Lord,
For now shall your life-long service
   Receive its endless reward.

" When I was an hunger'd, ye fed Me ;
   When thirsty, supplied My need ;
When I was a stranger, received Me ;
   When sick, ye were friends indeed.

" Ye came to Me in the prison,
  When I was an outcast one ;
Come, now, and behold My glory :
  Ye faithful servants, well done !"

Then the righteous, well remembering
  How poor their service has been,
Say, " Lord, when saw we Thee hungry,
  Or a stranger, and took Thee in ?

" Oh, what is our right, our Master,
  To be rewarded thus ?
We have done for Thee so little,
  But Thou hast done all for us."

And then shall the King make answer,
  Whatever the deed might be,
" For the least of these, my brethren,
  Ye did it unto Me."

LITTLE RAINY.

By the Author of "A Trap to Catch a Sunbeam."

ALL children, I believe, like stories about other
children, and perhaps some wet day when
you are tired of play you will like to read,
or have read to you, the history of a little child who
earned for herself the title of Little Rainy—can you
guess why? Because she was always crying—everything that vexed her caused showers of tears to fall
from her eyes; so that, instead of her own pretty
name of Mabel, she was called always Little Rainy.
She would have been a very pretty little girl, but for
this silly habit. If she had a lesson to learn, she
cried; if she could not fasten or unfasten her things,
she cried; if she lost anything, she cried; so that
soon her own pretty name of Mabel was quite for-
gotten, and she was known only as Little "Rainy"
everywhere.

Was it not silly? for she ought to have been
quite happy and merry; she had everything that
she could wish—toys of all kinds—a bright cheer-

ful home, loving parents, and brothers and sisters for companions ; but wherever she went, every one had to be warned of her foolish habit, and at length the kind friends who invited her brothers and sisters to all sorts of merry meetings, gave up asking her ; for they said it would be no pleasure to the poor child, she only cried and made every one else unhappy.

One bright summer day, a lady who had only just come to live in the neighbourhood, and had a large family of children of her own, called to ask Mrs Graham if she would let all her little folks join in a pic-nic.

"I always take the weather by surprise," she said, in her bright cheerful voice, which was quite a pleasure to listen to,—" so never *fix* a day for a pic-nic, but just look out of the window in the morning, and if the day looks hopeful, away we go."

"But I do not know what I have in the way of provisions," said Mrs Graham, smiling, " for my little ones to take."

"Never mind about that, a few berries and some of your delicious cherries will be quite sufficient for them to bring. Let me see how many are to come from here—ten ?"

"Oh! dear me," Mrs Graham answered, laughingly. "I think *five* quite enough, and out of that lot, Baby and Godfrey and Mabel "——

A pleading look from little Maude stopped the

words rising to her lips. She was just going to say, "Mabel cannot go, for fear she should cry," and Maude put her arm round her mother's neck, and whispered—

"Do let her go, mamma dear, this once. It will be so lonely and so sad for her to stay away from such a treat."

Mrs Graham liked to encourage her children in kindness to each other, and seldom therefore refused them when they asked any favour for one another. So she said aloud in answer to little Maude's whisper—

"Well, as you ask me, Maude, she shall go; but I must tell Mrs Stevenson not to be unhappy or alarmed if Mabel cries. I am sorry to say," she said, turning to her visitor, "that I have a foolish little girl who is always crying; at whatever she does not like, or any difficulty she meets with, she instantly cries, so that lately I have refused every invitation for her."

"Oh! poor little maid, but she will not cry to-day. I'm sure we will take care she is not distressed, won't we, Maude?" said Mrs Stevenson, kindly. "Run away and tell the rest, and get your things on, and come quickly, for the waggonette is to be at the door at half-past eleven."

"A waggonette! Oh! what delightful fun! and away ran little Maude, shouting up-stairs to the

others to make haste and come to her, she had such
news.   Of course, directly she entered the nursery,
toys and books were thrown aside to hear what she
had to tell, and instantly foolish Mabel began to cry.

"What is the matter *now*, Rainy?" said little
Bob, who, sitting astride the rocking-horse, with a
helmet made out of a newspaper, and a wooden
sword, had been "on duty" for some considerable
time before the Horse Guards,—"what's the matter
now?"

"You'll all go without me?" whined the poor
child, "and I should like to go in a waggonette, and
I never was at a pic-nic, and it is a shame."

"But you are going," said Maude, as soon as she
could make herself heard,—" you are going too, indeed you are.   Mamma says so."

And then silly little Mabel stopped her tears, and
ran off with the rest to get ready for this great treat;
and for the next ten minutes there was as much
noise and confusion as five children could possibly
make—indeed I may say ten, for each child made
noise enough for two,—Baby sharing in the general
hilarity, and taking advantage of the confusion to
seize a doll of Maude's, and bang its head on a
chair, to her own infinite delight, and the utter
destruction of poor Dolly's beauty.

Well, they are off at last, and nurse sits down
again in peace, thinking it quite a holiday to have

them all away for an hour or two; and Baby is in her glory too, in full possession of all the toys. Mistress of all she surveys, she trots about the nursery, pulling out all the furniture from the dollies' houses, disarranging all the dollies' beds and cradles, with happy little laughs of triumph to think how completely she has it all her own way, this little saucy usurper of toy kingdom! No rough little hands to snatch away in haste the plaything she has with so much trouble secured,—no loud angry cries of "O Baby! you nasty little thing! you've got my best doll," or "my beauty house." No, no, she can have them all now, and it is a real holiday to her as well as to the rest.

And away goes the waggonette, with its freight of happy children, along the high, dusty road first,— passing carts going to market, and the carrier's van, and one or two pony-chaises and dog-carts belonging to the neighbouring gentry; and all the occupants of the several vehicles give a pleasant smile to the little troop. Presently they turn down a lane, and the excitement increases. At the bottom of this lane is the wood where the cloth is to be laid, and the dinner eaten, and the glorious game of "Bears," and "Australian Settlers," and "Hide-and-seek," and "everything lovely," as mamma says, is to commence.

It is a wonderful road to travel, over such deep

K

ruts that they are bumped and shaken almost off their seats ; but that's nothing, it only makes more fun. And at length the gate of the wood is seen, and a loud cheer of delight rises through the air. Out they scramble, rushing through the gate, over the gate, under the gate, nobody could wait whilst another passed, all must of necessity rush in somewhere and somehow.

Then there is such a variety of opinions as to *where* they shall drive. Of course, every one has a different suggestion, but they are very willing to give up to kind Mrs Stevenson, who assured them she has fixed on a lovely spot ; so they race after her and the men bearing the hampers; and soon the contents are got out, and the cloth is laid, but Mrs Stevenson says they must not begin to eat just yet, for some one is coming,—some one whom they would be so sorry not to wait for. They are to guess who it is ; they make a great many bad guesses, and then Mrs Stevenson takes compassion on their curiosity, and tells them that she has asked Mr Tupper to come. Mr Tupper! who is he ? The little Grahams knew nothing about him ; but as all the other children shout for joy, they feel bound to do the same, and there is a tremendous noise for a few moments, the last sound of which has scarcely died away when the noise of wheels coming along the lane creates a fresh excitement. "Here he comes, run and meet him;" and up they all scrambled, and away they ran, all but two of them,—Mabel who is crying, and poor little, good, unselfish Maude, who is staying beside her to quiet and console her.

"What is the matter?" asks Mrs Stevenson, kindly.

"Mabel says she is so hungry," said Maude; "but please never mind, she always cries,—she will be quite right presently, indeed she will."

"But if it is only hunger," answered Mrs Stevenson, "we can happily soon stop that; here is a piece of cake, little maid."

"But then I shan't be able to eat my dinner; my mamma does not allow me to have anything before dinner," sobbed the foolish child.

"Dear, dear, this is a bad business," said Mrs Stevenson, smiling, "but as Mamma has confided you to my care to-day, I think I may give you leave to eat this piece of cake, and then you can run away after the others,—they are gone to meet one of the most charming men in the world, who, if you felt ever so much inclined to cry, would send all the tears away; so, quickly eat your cake and run off."

Somewhat gloomily still, Mabel took the offered slice of cake, and Maude said—

"Let us go after the others; you can eat it as we run," for she had a great curiosity to see this charming person, and was sure she should love him very

much if he could charm away Mabel's tears; so
with a little coaxing she persuaded her to follow the
rest of the party, carrying her cake with her; and
they were trotting along very happily when Maude
unfortunately said—

"I wonder if we shall be able to find our way?"

This was quite enough for Mabel, and down fell
the tears again.

"O Mabel dear! pray, pray don't cry any more!
It was only my fun; we shall be sure to find our
way,—it was so stupid of me to frighten you, but,
indeed, I did not think I should. Hark! I can
hear their voices; if we follow this straight path we
shall be sure to come to them."

But unhappily it was far easier to make Mabel's
tears flow than to stop them, and to Maude's shame
and distress, she was still sobbing when, the voices
growing louder and louder, the whole party appeared
in sight.

They were all hanging round a tall, fair young
man, whose progress was really impeded by their
anxiety to convince him of their affection. Cyril—
baby Cyril—was perched on his shoulder, to the
great envy of all the rest, but each had managed to
have hold of him,—his coat-tails satisfying two of
them.

"What's the matter?" he exclaimed, at sight of
the two little girls; "any one hurt?"

"No; she's always blubbering," said one of the boys. "I never saw such a little muff."

He was quickly reproved by his sister, some two years older than himself, the eldest, indeed, of all the little ones, who, like a true little lady, walked up to Mabel, who was hastily drying her eyes, and offered her a few wild-flowers she had gathered, and asked her if she had seen any coming along.

Poor Little Rainy, feeling very much ashamed of herself, said "No;" and then Minna, taking her hand, said—

"We two are going to run back—catch us who can;" and away they started, leaving little Maude, very grateful for Minna's kindness to her sister, to make acquaintance with Mr Tupper.

That was very easily done, and before they reached what the children called "the dining-room," Maude had seized a hand, disengaged for the moment, of the new comer, and was as much at home with him as all the rest.

Getting the cloth laid occupied them most agreeably for some time, and eating the dinner afterwards, perhaps, still more so; and when Mr Tupper produced from a basket some splendid fruit, the little rogues fell to again as though they had not had a mouthful.

"No more now," he exclaimed at last, "the rest is for tea;" and shutting down the lid of the basket

he seated himself upon it to prevent the possibility
of any one getting its contents, and said, "Now what
game is it to be? the little girls must choose first."

"Bears, and you be the great bear," was the
unanimous answer.

"Very well, I must turn myself into one first;"
and to their great astonishment he took off his hat,
his coat, and waistcoat, and took out of a carpet-
bag—which, with the hamper of fruit, he had had sent
to the wood—a large bear-skin rug.   This he fastened round him, and on his head he put a cap of
the same skin, and large fur gloves; and uttering a
long, low grunt, he rushed away amongst the trees.

"Now," said Minna, "we have all got to go out
in the wood, and pretend we are taking a walk,
and then we must hear him roar, and then we must
race home—this must be home."

"We ought to have settled home with him before
he started," said Bob.

"Yes, that would have been better, but we will
call out the 'dining-room' is home,—he will hear us,"
said Minna.   "What will you do, Mamma darling?"

"Stay here quietly with my book, and receive
you on your return."

"All right then, let us be off.   Shall I be the
mamma and Ellen the nurse, or will you be the
mamma, Maude?"

"Oh no! you be the mamma, you're the biggest."

" Very well then.   Cyril, you must be my little boy, and I am going to take you."

" Now, Nurse, you must meet me at—no, I think you had better bring the other children and come with me ; and you, my dear boys," she said, turning with a little matronly air to her brothers, " come too, and bring your guns ; I hear there are a great many bears in the wood."

" Bears ! then I give warning," said Ellen.

" Oh, nonsense, Ellen, that is not playing right ; is it, Mamma ? Nurses would not give warning directly because there were bears, would they ?"

" They might do so, Minna," said Mrs Stevenson, laughing, " but I have never been placed in such a position myself, so I cannot say."

" Well, they would have to come out if their mistress ordered them, anyway, because when they give warning they stay a month, so you must come, Ellen."

" Oh, very well, but I shall scream horribly if he growls."

" That will be better fun, come along," and away the children all trooped into the wood.   But at the first growl and dash out of the bushes from the supposed bear, Mabel burst into a passion of tears, and throwing herself down on the ground, refused to run with the rest to the home where they were to find refuge from the monster, although the children urged her with assurances of perfect safety there, in as glowing terms as though a wild beast were really in pursuit of them.

"It hurts me to run," she sobbed, "and I don't like playing at bears,—it makes me dream."

"Never mind," said dear, gentle little Maude, "you others run on, I will stay here with Mabel; don't, pray, let us spoil your game;" and as another loud roar was heard, and the furred figure was again seen issuing from his place of concealment, away ran the children, screaming at the top of their voices, leaving the foolish child and her kind sister beneath the tree where she had placed herself.

"I wish I hadn't come, I do; I'm spoiling your fun, and I'd give the world to be at home. It's so hot, and my head aches so," whined poor Little Rainy.

"Well, we won't play at the running games," said Maude. "Let us find some wild-flowers, and make a basket of sticks, and fill it; won't that be nice quiet fun? Don't cry any more, there's a dear," said the child, wiping away the tears with her own handkerchief; "you know Mamma will never let you come again, if she knows you've cried."

"But it is so much better fun to play altogether. I can play with you at home," said the fractious little girl.

"I daresay they'll be soon tired of this game, and

then we can play all together at something you'll like better," said Maude. "Come, let us go and find flowers."

Somewhat unwillingly, Mabel rose and followed Maude, and for a little while they amused themselves searching for flowers, though poor Maude would far rather have joined in the merry game which the shouts of the children assured her was still going on. Kind, good little girl, you may hope that the bright-eyed angels are rejoicing over you in this, to you, great act of self-denial and unselfish love.

Maude had twined together the rushes for her basket, and was filling it with moss, and getting quite interested in her employment, when Charlie Stevenson came running towards her.

"Oh ! here you are. Mamma says you are to come to her. She will take care of that little ' cry baby, and you can come and play."

"Oh, don't say "—— began poor Maude, but she was too late. Mabel had heard the word, and forgetting how she was justifying him for so calling her, she burst into a passionate fit of crying.

"I wish I was at home, I do,—nobody calls me names there," she sobbed.

"Yes, they do, they call you 'Rainy.' Ah, ah! I know. Ma' said so, and you wouldn't have been let to come, if Maude had not begged for you,—you 're always crying,—and you're crying now,—'cry baby, cry, put your fingers in your eye'"——

"Oh! hush, hush! do, pray," said little Maude, running to her little sister, and putting her arms around her. "You mustn't tease her, indeed we never do,—it only makes her worse."

"I'd tease her if she was my sister, till I broke her," said the little gentleman, grandly,—" but come along to Mamma."

"No, no!" screamed Mabel, clinging to Maude, and hiding her face in her neck. "I won't."

"Leave her alone, then, and you come," persisted Charlie.

"No, I'd rather not,—I'll wait with her; she will come presently."

"I'll make her! I'll carry her; I'm as strong as anything," said Charlie, preparing to prove his words; but before he could show the great strength of "anything" another spectator came on the scene.

Mr Tupper, looking very warm from his late exertions, without coat or waistcoat—only the fur cap remaining as evidence of the furious wild beast he had been pretending to be.

"What has happened? What is all this crying about?"

"Oh! this child does nothing but cry, Mr Tupper, and her sister cannot do anything with her; and O lor'! she is a regular bore," said Charlie.

" Indeed, young man ; then you of all people ought
to have patience with her, for you are subject to the
same complaint sometimes."

" I 'm sure I don't cry and whine," said Charlie,
sharply.

" No, but you 're a ' regular bore ' sometimes."

Charlie knocked the bloom off a primrose growing
near, and muttering something about going back to
the others, hurried away ; and Mr Tupper, seating
himself on the ground beside the little girls, said, lay-
ing his hand gently on Mabel,—

" Look here,—leave off crying. It spoils your eyes,
and does no good. Come with me,—I am going to tell
a story to the children while they rest, and you shall
sit on my knee. Come along." And raising her
gently but firmly from the ground, he took her up
in his arms, and bidding Maude follow, walked along
through the mazes of the wood, talking to Maude
until Mabel's sobs had quite ceased, and they found
themselves on the spot where they had dined, and all
the children with Mrs Stevenson seated in a circle.

" There they come ! A story, a story !" was the
joyful cry. " Here 's your seat, Mr Tupper," said
Minna. And after some little confusion as to who
was to sit next him, they finally settled themselves ;
and with eager eyes fixed on his face, and poor little
Mabel's head resting on his shoulder, he began as
follows :—

"A long while ago, a great way off, in a place a great many miles from everywhere, there lived a little boy. I daresay he had a papa and a mamma somewhere,· but I never heard anything about them, so I can't tell you ; all I know is about this little boy. Well, he was a fat, rosy-faced little fellow, and ought to have been as happy as the day was long, for he had everything to make him so, but somehow or other nothing was ever right with this young gentleman, and he always took to crying whenever anything put him out." There was an involuntary glance from all the children to little Mabel seated on Mr Tupper's knee, with her head still resting on his shoulder, but he answered by a look which instantly turned all eyes away, and he went on— "It was a very foolish thing of this little boy, for it made his eyes very weak and his nose very red, so that instead of being a pretty little chap, whom one would have liked to chuck under the chin and pelt with sugar-plums and sixpences, he was a poor, miserable, white-faced, red-nosed, wry-mouthed individual, one felt inclined to run away from as fast as possible. One day he was wandering about by himself in the lanes by his home—he played generally alone, for the other little boys could not bear to play with him ; he was sure, they said, ' to howl about something '—when he suddenly saw on a large dock-leaf the most beautiful butterfly he had ever

beheld. Taking off his cap, he approached cautiously
on tip-toe to make a captive of the beautiful insect,
but the bright eyes were too sharp for him, and
away it soared, now and then stopping and settling,
and then off again, on and on, the boy eagerly fol-
lowing, until at last he found himself on the banks of
a river, where he did not recollect ever having been
before. Well, what do you think he did ? Instead
of sitting down on the edge of the shore and throwing stones into the water, as any sensible boy would
have done, he began to cry and howl as loud as he
could. Close by where he stood there was a large
weeping willow, dipping its branches into the sparkling water, and as he paused for a second to get his
breath preparatory to another howl, he heard a very
loud sigh. He stopped crying instantly, startled at the
sound, for there was no one near him that he could
see ; even the butterfly was gone, and there was
no sign of life anywhere. He listened, and the sigh
was repeated louder—it certainly came from the
tree ; he looked up into its branches ; but no one was
there ; but presently he saw, peeping out of a
hole in the trunk, the tiniest of faces, about
the size of a tiny doll, and he heard a small puny
voice say, ' Little boy, what evil fate brought you
here ? I, like you, was once a little child in a bright
happy home, which I made wretched with my con-
stant tears and complainings ; and I was changed into

a weeping willow; and ever since, all children who cry or complain beside this tree, are punished by the River Fairy till they cease crying for anything.'

"Dumb with astonishment, the boy stared at the little face whilst it spoke, and at the tree when the face disappeared; and then, without stopping to consider which way he was to go, he took to his heels and ran off home as fast as he could. He said nothing of his adventure, because he did not think that any one would believe him, and that would have distressed him terribly; and all the rest of the day, as nothing happened to trouble him, he never cried, and so forgot all about the words he had heard, and the meaning conveyed in them.

"The next morning, as soon as he was dressed, he took his hoop out to play with it before breakfast, and was rolling it along very happily when a big baker's boy going by with a basket of bread gave the hoop a kick. A piteous howl issued from the silly boy's lips at once. The baker laughed loudly and went on; but when the foolish child stooped to pick up his hoop, what do you think? Why, there was nothing to be seen but a pool of water! Fancy his astonishment. He ran in-doors as fast as he could, and called everybody to tell what had happened. Naturally nobody believed it, but desired him to eat his breakfast, which was quite ready, and talk no nonsense; whereupon our friend again began to cry,—'it was so wicked not to believe him,' he whined; 'he knew he never did tell stories.' They let him cry; it was no use trying to comfort him; and as he was getting hungry, he stopped, intending to console himself with his bread and milk, but, to his horror and dismay, nothing was to be seen but a large basin of water! And so it was during the whole of the day, and for many days after. Whatever he took up or touched, if he cried, turned at once to water, until all his little property was gone. His paints all swam about in the box, a many-coloured pool—his tools melted into a lead-coloured liquid —his blocks dripped from their box in coloured spots—his puzzles were like muddy puddles, and his books pulpy masses, the print all blurred and unreadable—so that nothing remained to him of all his possessions but his little umbrella."

A shout of laughter from the children here interrupted Mr Tupper.

"Well done, River Fairy. Everything was so wet, he wanted an umbrella, they thought," said Minna.

"And a waterproof and goloshes, too," said Bob, "I should fancy."

"Don't interrupt stories, please," said the children.

"Well, but I can't go on much more, because it is a law of nature that when you get to the end you can't go any farther, and my story is drawing to its

close. The little boy, finding the extreme unplea-
santness of these moist playthings, made up his mind
to leave off his ridiculous and worrying habit ; and
his efforts were so brave and persevering, that he
was rewarded by a mysterious parcels' delivery cart
coming one day fairly loaded with good, solid, dry
presents for him; and still more, by the victory he
gained over himself. He was never known from that
day forth to cry any more—not even when he hurt
himself.

"Now, jump up," said Mr Tupper, rising, with Mabel
still in his arms, "and have a game at hares and
hounds. We're the hares,—I'm the papa hare, and
this is my baby. I shall drop cherries in my track."

"Hooray! all right," cried the children; and
Maude looked up in Mr Tupper's face, a whole
world of gratitude in her soft brown eyes, for the
tact with which he had spared her little sister any
allusions in the story, which was so evidently meant
as a lesson to her. They were soon full of the excitement of their play, and Mabel could not think
of a reason to cry, carried about so comfortably
in these kind, strong arms, every now and then
fed with a ripe cherry, with the pleasant, bright
face looking into hers ; and at length they were
caught ; and then tired and hot, they were all glad
once more to seat themselves beneath the trees, boil
the kettle in gipsy fashion, and have a "jolly" tea,

as Bob called it. A few riddles asked, and rhymes made, and a game at cross questions, and then the red glow of the setting sun gave warning to depart, and the tired but happy children scrambled up into the waggonette, and with a long, loud cheer, they left the wood on their homeward way. At first they joked and laughed and sung, but one by one the voices ceased, until at last Bob and Charlie had it all to themselves, and the girls began begging them not to make such an " awful noise."   As they neared home, Mabel began a slight whimper, she was " so tired," but Maude whispered with a smile, " Take care of the River Fairy," and Mabel checked her tears at once.

The nurse had been expecting a tiresome evening when the children returned, for when Mabel was tired, there was generally no knowing what to do with her; but to her surprise and delight, the little girl gave no trouble whatever, and they were all soon fast asleep, dreaming of woods and flowers and waggonettes.

A bright sunshine awakened the children in the morning, and they were glad to get up and make haste to dress, that they might tell " Mamma " all about yesterday, for she would not allow them to talk when they came home, they were so tired.

Maude cautiously avoided the story told by Mr Tupper, but Mabel said—

L

"Mamma, Maude has not told you all. Mr Tupper told us such a pretty fairy tale about a little boy who was always crying, so a river fairy came and turned all his toys to water. I shouldn't like that, but I often deserve it, don't I ? "

"Well, you do, certainly, my child. It is a sad habit, and I should be thankful to any fairy who would cure my little girl," said Mrs Graham.

"But fairies are not real, Mamma," said Mabel, " so I can't be cured."

"No, my child, fairies are not real, but these pretty tales have been written to amuse children, and give them a good lesson, which, because it amuses them, they never forget. When you think of the River Fairy, and the way she punished the foolish little boy, you will remember your own foolish habit, and strive to correct it; and, you know, my good little girl, Who to ask to help you to correct all silly faults."

Mabel made no answer, but she did not the less feel how right her mother was, and from that time forth made a resolution to break herself of this tiresome fault.

It was very difficult at first ; she had many failures. Many times she feared to look into her paintbox, or peep into the doll's house, from a dread to see that the River Fairy had been busy amongst her things—not, as she told Maude in confidence, that she "right down believed it, but still Mamma might get it done somehow as a punishment; for of course mammas can do everything, can't they, Maude?"

One morning, some weeks after the pic-nic, Mrs Graham said to her—

"Mabel, you have tried very hard, I can see, to master your faults, and Papa and I wish to encourage you. We have, therefore, determined to give you at Christmas something which I am sure will delight you immensely, if by that time you have *quite* conquered your faults; so go on bravely."

With a bright smile Mabel sprung from her chair, and kissed her mother fondly; and you may suppose how eagerly she ran to tell Nurse and her brothers and sisters the news.

Christmas was coming on fast, cold winds, frosts, and snows heralding the approach of the season so dear to all children. Mabel had been so good that every hope was entertained of her receiving her promised reward.

They were now expecting the boys home from school, and all was busy preparation for them. It had been Bob's first trial of school life, and therefore the four girls had an especial welcome for him, after this first separation. What a noise there was when they did arrive! Then, no doubt, you can imagine how every one's tongue ran at once, and what an incessant capering up and down stairs, and

in and out the garden there was; then they had to
be told of the present Mabel anticipated if she had
broken herself of her fault; when Bob imprudently
exclaimed—

"O lor'! she'll never get that," expecting, even
as he said, a howling from the poor child.

The surprise, therefore, was great when she only
said, very brightly—

"Ah, you'll see, Master Bob! Papa says 'Rome was
not built in a day'; but patience and perseverance
and trying made a great city at last, and you'll see
what I shall do."

"I'm sure she will succeed," said Maude, kissing
her; "and you must not discourage her."

Bob laughed, but said no more; and the time
went on. It wanted but a week to Christmas. The
present was to be given on Christmas Eve, and
Maude, dear, good, little Maude's anxiety exceeded
even her sister's.

All had gone well, up to the very last day, when,
as ill-luck would have it, it was too cold and damp
for the children to go out, and Master Bob's temper
was somewhat injured by his being kept in-doors.
They had been playing at a variety of noisy games,
and Mabel, getting tired, proposed to play at ladies
and gentlemen, with the dolls for babies.

Bob indignantly refused; and on being urged,
seized Mabel's doll, and threw it to the other end

of the room, the poor little waxen head dropping from its shoulders with the fall.

Maude uttered a cry of horror, and flew to Mabel, expecting to hear the customary dreadful cry; but, to her great surprise and delight, she only saw two large tears standing in her eyes, which were fixed on Bob with a look of piteous reproach.

"Oh! I say, Mabel, I am sorry; I am—don't cry, don't; here's all my money, you shall have another doll. Oh! I am so sorry," said the boy, all his bad temper gone at once.

Mabel, with a great effort to command her voice, said—

"No, no, Bob, you did not mean to break it; never mind; perhaps I can manage to mend it."

At this moment the door opened, and Mrs Graham entered. The children were loud in their apologies for Bob and praises of Mabel; and Mrs Graham took her by the hand, and kissing her, said—

"This is so perfect a proof that you have managed to conquer yourself, that I shall at once give you the promised reward, which I hope will console you for this sad accident to Dolly. You may come, Maude dear, too."

The children entered their mother's room together, and with speechless delight they beheld a perfect doll's house, which Mrs Graham opened, and displayed each room filled with most beautiful furniture, with curtains and spring blinds; Nurse, Cook, housemaids, footmen, all employed in their separate duties; the nursery furnished with every convenience, even to a swing for the children, of whom there were four; in short, each room was perfect, and, as Mrs Graham assured them, would occupy many hours to examine thoroughly.

You, my dear little ones, for whom this tale is written, can imagine how happy Mabel was, and I hope you have been sufficiently interested in her to be glad to know that from that time the old name of "Little Rainy" was exchanged for the far prettier one of "Merry Mabel."

THE CHILDREN'S WARD.

By the Editor.

HERE are many sorts of wards, just as there are many sorts of locks. I do not at all doubt that the first thing you will want to know, when you turn to this page, will be what is meant by "The Children's Ward."

I have so much to tell you that I shall not speak —I mean *write*—about the different sorts of wards, but will tell you at once that "The Children's Ward" means the *room* in which children are guarded, or taken care of.

Then next, you will want to know what "The Children's Ward" is about. Well, it is about a number of poor little children of whom I can tell you a lot of tales, some of them funny, some of them sad, but all such as I think you will like.

Most young people—and I must say, most grown-up people too—like to know what a book or a tale is about before they read it, or hear it read ; and as little patients have little patience, I will now tell you where "The Children's Ward" is, and all about it.

"The Children's Ward" of which I have to tell— for I hope there is a children's ward in many other towns—is in the General Infirmary at Leeds, in Yorkshire.

An infirmary is a hospital for persons who are infirm, that is, weak through disease or bodily injury. All infirmaries are hospitals, though all hospitals are not infirmaries—just as all birds are animals, though all animals are not birds.

Hospitals are buildings in which homes are provided by charitable persons for those who are in need. Christ's Hospital in London is a large school ; it is commonly called the Blue Coat School, because the scholars wear blue coats, such as were worn in the reign of King Edward VI. When the school was founded for the children of the poor, Greenwich Hospital was founded for disabled sailors, Chelsea Hospital for disabled soldiers ; and in all parts of Great Britain there are hospitals in which old people live rent-free, and have a sum of money allowed them. In some cases the allowance is large enough to pay for all they need, in others it is only a help towards their support.

There are institutions which, though they be *infirmaries*, are commonly called *hospitals;* for instance, St George's Hospital, Guy's Hospital, and Middlesex Hospital, in London.

From what I have told you, you will see that hospitals are not all intended for the *infirm* only ; but all infirmaries are intended for none but the infirm. The Infirmary at Leeds is called "general," because persons suffering from injuries or any sort of diseases, except those which are contagious, or "catching," such as small-pox, are admitted into it. It is by some said to be "the finest hospital in Europe."

Now for a short tale—an anecdote. A gentleman who spent much of his time in district visiting, called on a poor woman. Amongst her other troubles she had one of her children afflicted with sore eyes. The gentleman asked her if she had taken the child to a surgeon. "Oh yes, please, sir," she replied ; and after a long story of what he said and what she said, and what she had done to get her child cured, added, "Could you, sir, give me a 'recommend' to the Iron Foundry ? "

" The Iron Foundry ! " exclaimed the gentleman. " What iron foundry do you mean ? and what recommendation do you want ? " " Why, sir, Dr. Brown *teld* me to get a *recommend* for the Iron Foundry, and take my Billy there."

The gentleman had heard that water in which iron is suddenly plunged is sometimes used as a lotion, but he did not know that it was good for sore eyes. After a few moments' thought he asked, " Who is Dr Brown ? " " Please, sir, he's the gentleman *as* keeps the doctor's shop at the corner of *this* *'ere* street." " Well, and what iron foundry do you wish to take your child to ? "

From her answer the gentleman discovered that she meant the *Eye Infirmary!* *Doctor* Brown was not even a surgeon ; he was only a chemist and druggist who kept a very small shop in a poor neighbourhood.

You see all infirmaries are not *general.* An "eye infirmary," for instance, is only for complaints or injuries of the *eyes.*

The General Infirmary at Leeds was instituted more than a hundred years ago, in the year 1768. I cannot tell you on what month it was opened, but I can tell you that in that year the number of *in-patients* was *seventy-six.*

Another anecdote. A district visitor, a lady, called on a poor woman whose daughter was ill. The girl was not in danger, nor yet in great pain, but she was very peevish and fretful, and gave her poor mother " a world of trouble." She would not wait for any little thing she wanted, though she could do very well without it ; her mother had to leave off whatever she was doing as soon as it was the whim of her daughter to want something. The lady knew this well, and one day when the girl

called to her mother repeatedly to bring her something she asked for, the lady said to her, "My dear
child, you must not be impatient." The mother
heard it, and, beckoning the lady aside, said in a
low tone of voice, so that the daughter should not
hear : "She can't help being impatient ; she was so
all the time she was in the hospital. She was taken
in there as impatient at once, and though the
doctors said when she come out, she had *no call* to
be impatient *no longer*, I think *they was wrong.*"
The poor woman mistook the word *in*-patient for
*im*patient !

My readers, of course, know the difference between " in-patients " and " impatience," and I need
scarcely tell them that many an *in*-patient is *im*-
patient too ; but it may be well to tell them that
those only who sleep in an infirmary are *in*-patients ;
others who go for advice and medicine are *out*-
patients.

When I say that only patients who sleep in an
infirmary are in-patients, I mean those who are
provided with beds in the infirmary, for many a
patient is in too much pain to sleep.

There are always very many more out-patients
than there are in-patients. In the first year of the
General Infirmary at Leeds, the number of out-
patients was a hundred and fifty-five, that is twice
seventy-six and two over ; so the number of out-

patients was in the first year more than double that
of the in-patients. In the next year, there were
nearly five times as many out-patients as there
were in-patients. There has never since that year
been such a great difference between the number of
in-patients and that of out-patients. Many of the
out-patients are little children—some too young to
walk. If I were asked to "guess" the number of
children who are out-patients compared with the
number who are in-patients, I should say four or
five to one ; that is, for every poor little child that is
in the children's ward, there are five who are taken
to the Infirmary several times a week for the doctors
to see.

I ought, perhaps, to tell you that the patients do
not have to pay for doctors' advice or for medicine.
The in-patients, children as well as grown-up persons, are also provided with all the food they need.
All the wards are fine rooms,—finer than some
town-halls,—they are kept very clean, and so are all
the things that are in them. The patients have kind
nurses to wait upon them and take care of them all
night as well as all day.

Of course, the things wanted in an infirmary
must be paid for. A great deal of money is
wanted, and the more money the gentlemen who
manage the infirmary get, the more good they can
do with it. About this we shall have more to say

by and by, for I know you will soon want another anecdote or short tale.

I think, though, you will not be sorry if you give attention to what I am now going to tell. It is very interesting, though it will not draw tears to your eyes, nor make a little lump rise in your throat, neither will it make your sides ache with laughing. You know very well that there is much you like to read about, or to be told about, that does nothing of that sort.

I am going to tell you a little more—a very little more about the number of patients.

In the year 1769, of which I have already told you something, the number of in-patients was 116, so that if there had been two more, there would have been half as many again as there were in the year before. In the next year—the year 1770—there were 159 in-patients, and 675 out-patients; so that the whole number of patients was 834.

I think I shall surprise you. I have told you the number of patients in the year *seventeen* hundred and seventy; I will now tell you the number in the year *eighteen* hundred and seventy, it was *ten thousand and forty-four!* Of this large number *two thousand five hundred and forty-eight* were in-patients.

Some young folks are very fond of figures—I mean making calculations—and even working by

mental arithmetic what some would call "hard"
sums. Others like any school work better than
arithmetic. But lest you should think I am about
to "lecture" you, and tell you to be good children
and learn your lessons, and all that sort of thing,
which is in its way excellent advice, I will tell you
a short story. Just let me say a few words first.
Don't suppose for one moment that I think young
folks do not, at times, need the sort of advice to
which I have alluded. But "there is a time for all
things." This is the time to talk about little convalescents.

Now for the story. A young lady—a little convalescent—was one day reading an interesting
report of a charitable institution for children.

"I think, my dear," said her papa, "you might
be a subscriber of a half-guinea."

"Oh, papa! I should very much like to do so if
I could."

"Well, I think you can," was Papa's reply.

"How can I, dear papa? it is so seldom I have
a half-sovereign of my own, and a half-guinea is
a half-sovereign and sixpence."

"You are quite right," said her Papa. "I am
glad to find you know the difference between a half-
guinea and a half-sovereign; did you ever see a
half-guinea?"

"Yes, Papa; the last time I was at Grandmamma's she showed me one that she had kept ever since she was a little girl no older than I am. I think she said one of her aunts gave it to her when it was quite new and bright, as a new-year's gift, and told her that as long as she kept it she would never be without money ; and Grandmamma said that would have been quite as true if it had been an old farthing ! She also showed me a guinea that was given to her some years afterwards, because she had so carefully kept her bright half-guinea."

"Ah !" replied Papa, " I have seen those coins many a time and had many a lesson taught from them. Some of them I will repeat to you if you ask me when I have a little time to spare."

"Now, dear Papa," said the little convalescent; " you know it is a long time since I have had any lessons to learn ; it would be quite a treat to me to hear you *recapitulate,* as we say at school, one of the lessons you learnt so long—very long ago. Do, please, at once ' *make time,*' as you sometimes say you do."

"Well, then," said Papa, " I do not promise to repeat word for word any of the lessons I had on those coins ; but as you wish it, I will repeat one of the lessons *in substance;* that is, I will state the ideas in nearly, if not exactly, the same words :—

" ' My dear boy, I own that I am often proud of having kept these coins so many years. But

treasuring them has cost me many, many pounds,
much self-denial, and often sad thoughts as well.
When I was a girl I had as much pocket-money as
most of my age and station in life. I do not wish
to boast, but I must say few of my young friends
did more good with pocket-money than I did. I
am sure I found more pleasure in spending it—I
mean a good portion of it—in helping the poor,
than they did in spending it all in bazaars or toy-
shops, or at pastrycooks' or confectioners' shops—
in short, in spending it on themselves and on
those who who were not in need. Often my
half-guinea gave me trouble. Often I had only
a shilling, or even less, when I wanted to give
away a few shillings; then I thought I would
change my half-guinea. But I was asked to keep
it as long as I could. What was I to do? So one
day I asked my mamma whether I had not better
get it changed for silver coins, and keep a bright
shilling or sixpence instead—that would be *part* of
the half-guinea, the other part would provide food
or clothing for some poor child; what was the use
of money locked up in a box? My mamma said it
was a very proper feeling, and she was glad to find
me so thoughtful, but she said I ought to regard
that half-guinea as though it were a trinket or a
mere ornament or curiosity which cost, or might be
sold for ten shillings and sixpence. She pointed to

other presents which I had received, and which could have been sold for much more than my little gold coin was worth. " Would you like to part with them," she asked. Of course, I said I should not. " Well then, you should think no more of this half-guinea as *money*, but as a coin kept, not only as you will keep it, in affectionate remembrance of the giver, but also as a curiosity, for it is sure to be a curiosity if it is kept a great number of years, with as much care as it is now kept."

" 'I do not wish you to act like a miser—to hoard money for the mere sake of hoarding it. But there are exceptions to every rule. You can soon give in charity as much as this coin is worth, if, from your pocket-money, you take only a few pence a week from what you spend on what you can very well do without !'

" There now ! " said Papa, " I think I have repeated my lesson very fairly."

" You have, indeed, dear Papa ! " replied the little girl, " and I thank you very much. I have learnt a lesson too."

" What is that, my child ? " asked Papa.

" It is that, by putting by a little of my pocket-money every week—so little that I should scarcely miss it—and I should have no need to give away less than I do now, I should be well able to subscribe a

M

half-guinea at the end of the year. Let me see—a penny a week would be fifty-two pence, equal to four shillings and fourpence a year. Twice that would be eight and eightpence : one halfpenny more a week would make it ten shillings and tenpence. Why! only twopence-halfpenny a week makes *more* than a half-guinea a year. Oh, Papa! I can even well spare fivepence a week, so I can subscribe a guinea a year. I'll have a little box and put sixpence in it every week, then I shall at the end of the year have a guinea, and five shillings over ! "

There are many persons who, from sheer want of *thought*, do not subscribe to such institutions as infirmaries. It is not from want of means. It would be well if there were a charity-box in every family, a *home* charity-box, as well as a missionary-box. Many a guinea subscription to *home* charities might be collected in that way.

A farmer's wife went to a missionary meeting in a village National school. She was pleased with what she heard from the different speakers. When the meeting was over, she went up to the clergyman and said, " Sir, I'm not one of those rich folks that give a guinea a year, but I'll give sixpence a week "!

It is almost time we went back to the General Infirmary at Leeds. It was looking over the " One

Hundred and Third Annual Report " of it, that led me to speak about calculation and "figures." The Report contains some very interesting tables.

My dear little *im*patients, don't be alarmed! I am not going to bring before you whole columns of figures. Well enough I know that the *tables* most interesting to you are dining-tables, breakfast-tables, and tea-tables.

The *tables* in the report would, it may be, prove less attractive to you than the multiplication-table, and other school-book tables. But for all that, the tables in the report are interesting to *some*, of whom I am one.

Shall I describe one of the most interesting of the tables? Methinks I hear a little voice exclaim, " Oh dear! the very thought of such a thing makes me feel sleepy."

Just " wait a wee ; " I do not mean to describe the subject of the table, only its appearance. It fills two opposite pages, and consists of columns and rows of figures ; each column has a " heading." Well, on *each* of the two pages there are *nineteen columns* of figures, so there are thirty-eight columns of figures, each column more than fifty figures deep !

This short description is, I imagine, quite enough for you. A " sum," in " compound proportion," or the conjugation of a French irregular verb, would " charm " you more than such a *table*. Now, don't you think it would ? I can guess the sort of answer you are ready to give. Sums and conjugations have but few "charms" for little learners, and fewer still for little convalescents.

But though the *table* would not interest you, I am sure that a few *facts* which it shows will. It shows that in the year 1870, the expenses of the Infirmary amounted to more than *thirteen thousand pounds* above what they amounted to in the year 1770, just a hundred years before ! It shows that in the year 1776, the income did not amount to *one* thousand pounds, and that ninety years afterwards, in the year 1866, it amounted to more than *eighteen* thousand pounds !

What has been said about *guineas,* reminds me of an interesting calculation which I made from a *table* in another part of the report.

I find that the annual subscriptions for the year 1870, would have been nearly *two hundred pounds less,* if most of the subscribers had given pounds instead of guineas !

Two hundred pounds, all from "odd shillings !" What a great deal of good can be done for poor little suffering children with two hundred pounds !

In the year 1870, there were more than eighteen hundred subscribers of a guinea and upwards, the largest annual subscription being *forty-one guineas,* or *forty-three pounds one shilling.*

But "the smallest donations are thankfully received." One district visitor collected more than two pounds ten shillings in *halfpenny* subscriptions ; another collected a guinea, and another a pound, in *halfpenny* subscriptions! One person collected during the year *nine pounds eighteen shillings* in *penny* subscriptions! Two thousand three hundred and seventy-six pennies!

The souls, as well as the bodies, of the in-patients are cared for. There is a clergyman of the Church of England paid to devote all his time to the in-patients, to pray with them every morning, and to minister on the Lord's Day, and on other occasions, in a chapel which forms part of the building.

It is not often, then, there are many in-patients attending the chapel services, for as soon as they are well enough to leave their beds and walk about, they are "discharged," so as to make room for others. If they are not quite well, and the doctors can do anything more for them, they are made out-patients. The Infirmary is always nearly full, and would be quite full, if it were not that a few beds must be kept ready so that, any hour in the day or night, patients can be admitted.

The chapel services are attended by officers, and by nurses, and other servants of the institution ; and also by some who take an interest in it, so that sometimes there is a full congregation.

Besides the chaplain, there are Scripture readers and town missionaries, who, as part of their duty, have to visit the in-patients on certain days. Then, again, there are ladies and gentlemen who visit them, read to them, and distribute tracts amongst them.

The Children's Ward is for the very youngest of the in-patients : there are generally children in the other wards.

I am now going to tell you about a poor little blind girl who was a patient in one of the women's wards.

On Sunday mornings, before the time appointed for divine service in the chapel, the chaplain holds a "Sunday class" in his room. When the little blind girl was well enough to walk about, the chaplain asked her if she would like to come to the class. She did not know. The chaplain tried to explain to her the object of the Sunday class, but he soon found that the poor girl was "blind" in more senses than one. She knew nothing of "the true light;" she did not even know the name of Him who is "the Light of the world!" She was as ignorant of the light of the Gospel as though she had been born and brought up amongst heathens! She had not heard of God,—she knew nothing about a Saviour,—she had not heard of such a place as heaven!

"How sad!" you will say; and so the chaplain thought. But he also thought, "Can it be possible that a girl of her age—ten years or more—brought up in such a town as this, in Christian Britain, the land of Bibles — a town in which churches, chapels, and schools, and ministers, and teachers abound,—can it be possible that all these things are hid from the eyes of her mind? Is she as *blind* as she seems to be?" Then, again, he thought, "It may be she does not understand my questions; I will try some other way with her."

"You know," said he, "that some day you must die, do you not?"

"No, sir!"

"No! Have you never heard of *death*?"

"No, sir!"

"What! Have you never lost by death any one you loved or knew? Have you never heard of any one who *died*?"

"Oh yes, sir!" and the face of the poor girl quite brightened. The chaplain, too, was pleased that at last he had an opening that he might let in more light.

"Well," said he, "tell me what you know about it—who was it who died?"

"A woman down our street, sir, she *dyed* an old gown!"

I can quite understand, my dear young friends,

that you "cannot help laughing" at such an answer. I own I laughed when the chaplain told it to me, and he laughed too. But I can quite as well understand that he did not laugh, nor even smile, when the answer was given to him. And, fond as you and I are of fun, we should have been more shocked than amused when the poor blind girl gave such an answer after saying that she knew nothing about God or heaven.

The chaplain was grieved and puzzled—puzzled to know how to begin to teach the poor girl. After thinking for a few moments, he said, " Do you know what a *fly* is ? "

" Yes, sir."

" Now, if there were a fly on this floor, and I were to put my foot on it and crush it—crush it so that there was nothing of it left that could be seen—what would you say of it ? "

As he spoke thus, he stamped on the floor, and drew his foot as though in the act of killing the fly.

The answer quite surprised him, and forced him to smile—and no wonder ; it was this :—"If you left *nowt* * of it, what could I say of *nowt ?* "

This sharp answer proved to the mind of the chaplain that the poor blind girl was not " dull " or "stupid." She was utterly ignorant of all that a child in a Christian land should know.

* *Nowt* is an old English way of pronouncing *nought*, " nothing." It is still used by the common people in Yorkshire.

I could tell you a great number of such tales, and so could almost any one who has visited much amongst the poor. There are thousands of grown-up people in England who know nothing, or very little indeed, about God. They cannot read, they will not enter any place of worship, nor will they listen to any one who wishes to speak about God, until they, through injury or disease, become inmates of an infirmary; or through old age and poverty, inmates of a workhouse; or worse still, through crime, become inmates of a prison. It is sad—very sad.

But it is cheering to know that the gospel seed sown in the infirmary often falls on good ground, and brings forth fruit. I remember two other anecdotes told me by the chaplain—one about a little boy, the other about a little girl.

The chaplain had spoken to the little boy about prayer, and he quoted the words of the Lord: "If two of you shall agree on earth as touching any-thing that they shall ask, it shall be done for them of my Father which is in heaven. For where two or three are gathered together in my name, there am I in the midst of them." A few days afterwards the little boy said to the chaplain, "You told me the other day that Jesus is with two or three when they pray; I have found out that He is with *one* who prays."

Cheering it is to a sufferer to be told that Jesus is near, still more cheering it is to feel that He is present—to find out for one's self that He is ever near!

The little girl of whom the chaplain told me was very young, and really a beautiful child. But pleasing as were her looks, more so were her simple and artless words. Her father, a rough sort of man, such as few of my young readers would care to speak to, came one visiting-day to see her. As he was going away, he met the chaplain, and spoke to him. The big, rough man, who seldom or never went to a place of worship, or cared to hear about God, was as gentle as a lamb. His little daughter had been telling him of what she had heard of the love of Jesus, and asking him if he was one who loved the Lord Jesus Christ.

As he spoke, his looks and the tone of his voice, more than his words, made known to the chaplain that he felt grieved he had lived so long "without God in the world."

It is to be hoped that the words of his little daughter, whom he dearly loved, made a lasting impression on his mind.

Ignorance is the cause of much misery and much pain. Many poor little children suffer greatly through the ignorance of their parents, or of those who take charge of them—for it cannot be said they take *care* of them.

I dare say most of you, when you were ill, wanted—or I should say *asked for*—and thought you *wanted*, things that were not good for you to have. There are many things that are very nice, and very good too, for those who are well, and even for some who are ill, but which to others who are ill would do much harm—as much harm, perhaps, as poison. This may seem strange to you, but any doctor, and indeed any well-educated person, will tell you that it is quite true.

It is not at all strange that young folks when they are ill, ask to have such things as they liked very much when they were well. And if such things can be had, no doctor, or parent, or friend will refuse to let them be had, unless there is some very good reason for refusing; in other words, unless such things will do harm to the patients.

Doctors are not at all fond of saying what diet a patient is to have. They seldom do so, unless there is good reason why they should.

I have heard of a lady who often sent for the doctor, though she was not at all ill—but she *said* she was ill; and had the doctor told her that there was nothing at all the matter with her, she would have been sure to send for another doctor. Knowing this, the doctor humoured her whim, felt her pulse, looked at his watch, asked her to let him see her tongue, shook his head, heard all she chose to tell, wrote a prescription, took his fee and his leave, got into his carriage, and enjoyed "the joke," as well as his ride. The "stuff" he prescribed for the lady could do her *no harm!*

One day she sent for him ; it was only to ask what she was to eat ! "Anything you please, madam," said he, " except the fire-irons or the fender —they will be hard to digest !" The lady did not send for a doctor till many years afterwards.

Do not suppose that doctors do not care what their patients eat or drink. When a doctor says, " Let the patient have whatever he (or she) fancies," he believes the patient to be a sensible person, or to be under the care of sensible persons, and that no-thing unwholesome or unfit for an invalid would be asked for or given.

A little boy—I knew him—was very ill. He took very little food. All sorts of nice things were brought to him to tempt him to eat. His poor mamma did all she could to coax him to eat, but in vain. He was a great favourite of the doctor, who also tried to induce him to " take nourish-ment."

One day the doctor and the mamma were sitting by the bedside of the little patient.

· " Doctor Davies," said he, " may I have some *carrot-pie?*"

"Carrot-pie !" exclaimed the doctor. " Do you

like it ?"—and he looked at the mamma, then at the patient, then at Mamma again.

"Well, sir," said the little boy, "I like carrots—and I like pie. I should think a carrot-pie would be very nice."

The doctor laughed, and so did the mamma. The doctor had never heard of such a thing as a carrot-pie—he was too polite to laugh when carrot-pie was first mentioned—he thought it might be a specimen of Mamma's domestic cookery, or something that Cook "made out of her own head." But poor Mamma had never manufactured, or caused to be mauufactured, such a pie ; and had her little son asked for a *pebble-pie*, she could not have been more surprised.

After a long illness, the little boy got quite well, and many a laugh he joined in about *carrot-pie*. I think it was ten or twelve years after he had first asked for carrot-pie, he wrote to his mamma, from some part of England, where he was travelling, that he had partaken of some. I forget in what county it was. In the county of Cornwall all sorts of things are made into pies. I mean all sorts of eatable things—not such things as pebbles or broken bottles.

There are many things that you often have, and think very nice, that are not known even by name to the children of the poor. But on the other hand, they think it a treat to have some things that you would not eat, unless you were very hungry indeed, and could get nothing else.

The diet of patients in an infirmary is very plain, but it is good, and every one has sufficient. They do not get pies or tarts, or asparagus, or green pease, or cauliflower, or even Windsor beans ; they get nothing, except in very special cases, that is expensive, or that requires much time and trouble to prepare. The managers are quite right to take care that the money they get is spent in such a way that as much good as possible is done with it. It would be a waste of money to spend it on things that patients can do very well without.

But *you* know that patients, and especially convalescents, and still *more* especially *little* convalescents, have all sorts of whims and fancies. If you were to wish for some out-of-the-way dainty—*carrot-pie*, for instance—mamma, or nurse, or whoever it is who takes care of you, would ask the doctor if you might have it. But many of the poor people who have children ill, are not so thoughtful. If it is in their power, they give the children whatever they ask for, and often they have what does them harm. Even grown-up persons will eat and drink such things as they well know are not good for them. They dread the doctor finding out what they have been eating and drinking.

I tell you all this because it may be that when you take an interest, as I trust you will, in a "Children's Ward," and you speak to some poor ignorant woman about it, you may hear that an infirmary is a shocking place for children to be in, because they don't like the food, and the doctors will not allow food to be brought to patients by their friends.   Then you will be able to tell her why it is so, and that doctors know best what is good for their patients.   You may tell her too of some little girl or boy who you knew had, when ill, to live on very plain diet, though his or her friends could afford to get any dainties the patient asked for.

Though patients do not in an infirmary get all sorts of nice things, many of them, I think I may say most of them, live better there than they do when they are at home.   Some things much liked by the poor are unwholesome, and sometimes good food is made unwholesome by the way in which it is cooked.

A doctor called to see a poor woman who was very ill at her own home.   Just before he came, a kind friend had visited and given her money to get a nice steak or chop.   She was frying it when the doctor come in.   "Now, my good woman," said he, "you must not eat that!   *Fried* meat will do you more harm than good ; you can give it to some one

who is in need, but in good health and *strong.*
Here, take this," he put a shilling in her hand, "and
get some of the same sort of meat for yourself, but
broil it, or cook it before the fire, do not *fry* it."

The doctor was not at all a *rich* man. He was
a "parish doctor," that is, a doctor paid by the
parish to give advice to the sick who were too poor
to pay a doctor. I knew him slightly, I sometimes
met him in the abodes of the poor amongst whom
I visited. Only a day or two before I was told by
the Scripture reader of the kind act which I have
just related, I called at a house in my district
where there was a sick person. Whilst I was
sitting by the bedside of the patient the "parish
doctor" came in. I rose to go, but the doctor
begged me not to do so. He knew I had just come,
and his visit would be very short, for he had
many more calls to make.

When he had done with the patient, he had a
little pleasant talk with me, and went away.

"You find him a very kind, pleasant gentleman,
do you not ?" said I to those in the room.

"Ah, sir, he may seem so to you, but he's very
rough with us poor folks," was the reply. Then I
was told how cross he was with Mrs Brown for
letting her little girl play in the street when she
ought to have been kept in the house ; how he
scolded poor Jones only "'*cause* he would drink

beer ; what he'd been used to all his life ;" and so on.

You will do well to bear in mind that ingratitude is often the result of ignorance. Many of the patients in an infirmary are very ignorant, and, therefore, many of them are ungrateful. The kind persons who support such institutions know this ; the kind doctors who without any payment give as much attention to the poorest person in an infirmary as they do those patients who are wealthy and can pay handsome fees, know this. But it makes no difference to them. They do not do kindness for the sake of getting thanks. If a fellow-creature is suffering pain, and in need, they think it their duty to afford what relief they can.

If you meet with ingratitude or even rudeness from poor ignorant people to whom you have been kind, it is no reason why you should cease to be kind.

Do not suppose that all the poor, or that all the very ignorant poor, are ungrateful. Far, far from it. Amongst grown-up infirmary patients as well as amongst poor parents and friends of those who are in, or have been in, " The Children's Ward," there are very many who are truly grateful. There are some who, as soon as they can, give proof of their gratitude by subscribing and inducing others to subscribe to the institution.

N

I intended telling you a great deal about some of the poor little sufferers in " The Children's Ward;" but whilst I was selecting some cases which were most likely to interest you, I received a nice contribution for this little book from one who is, amongst young readers, a favourite author. I did not wish you, my dear young friends, to lose the opportunity of reading or hearing a cheery tale; so to make room for it, I keep back from the printers what else I have written about "The Children's Ward." If you wish it, I may some day write a little book all about " The Children's Ward."

My greatest encouragement to write such a book would be to know that some of my young friends who read these pages, will do what they can to support " The Children's Ward."

Oh, I am sure if you could but see the poor little things—some of them not two years old—lying on beds of suffering, your hearts would ache for them. It is a sight you would not soon forget.

The patients in " The Children's Ward " suffer much ; but all that can be done for their comfort, is done. There are in all our large towns very many poor little children who cannot be admitted into a Children's Ward. Those who have charge of them are too poor to buy them what they require, and too ignorant to nurse them properly.

If there were more Children's Wards, and if those

already established were better supported, how
many a life might be saved, how many tears might
be dried, how many a heart now bowed down with
sorrow might be filled with gratitude and joy!

Think, my dear young friends, of God's goodness
to you ; think of the many blessings you enjoy, of
the many mercies which a loving and gracious
Father has bestowed on you, and I am sure I need
say no more on behalf of "The Children's Ward."—
FREELY YE HAVE RECEIVED, FREELY GIVE.

PRINTED BY BALLANTYNE AND COMPANY
EDINBURGH AND LONDON

www.ingramcontent.com/pod-product-compliance
Lightning Source LLC
Chambersburg PA
CBHW020614030726
47497CB00007B/2243